DUETS

DUETS

Per Brask & George Szanto

COTEAU BOOKS

Cover painting, "Romance," oil on paper, 1981, by Jane Zednik.

Cover and book design by Joyce Sotski.

Typeset by Type Systems, Regina.

Printed and bound in Canada by Hignell Printing Limited, Winnipeg.

The authors would like to thank David Arnason for editing this book.

Per Brask would like to thank the University of Winnipeg for its support of this project.

All quotes on pruning in "Tending the Garden" are from *Pruning Handbook* written by Lee Klein and published by Lane Books, Menlo Park, Calif., 1972.

George Szanto would especially like to thank Eugene Lion.

The publisher gratefully acknowledges the financial assistance of the Saskatchewan Arts Board, the Canada Council, the Department of Communications and the Manitoba Arts Council.

Canadian Cataloguing in Publication Data

Szanto, George, 1940-

Duets

ISBN: 1-55050-000-7

1. Short stories, Canadian (English)*. 2. Canadian fiction (English) - 20th century*. I. Brask, Per K., 1952-. II. Title.

PS8587.Z368D8 1989 C813'.01'08 C89-098080-2

PR9199.3.S936D8 1989

coteau books

Suite 209, 1945 Scarth Street
Regina, Saskatchewan
S4P 2H2

For

Geoffrey Andrew
(1906-1987)

and

Jan Brask
(1956-1988)

CONTENTS

I	*SENSE* — Szanto	3
	SUICIDE NOTE — Brask	18
II	*ON CHEEMY POND* — Szanto	25
	THE MOON — Brask	35
III	*SOCCER MADE IN GERMANY* — Brask	41
	THE YEAR THE LEAVES WERE SMALLER — Szanto	47
IV	*THE MAN WHO LOST NOUNS* — Szanto	61
	DEVILS — Brask	74
V	*ON THE QUEEN'S BIRTHDAY* — Brask	83
	SKULL — Szanto	88
VI	*FERRY* — Szanto	103
	SEEKING THE BOTTOM, AGAIN — Brask	110

VII *WHERE FAIRY GODMOTHERS COME FROM* . . 119
Szanto
TENDING THE GARDEN 135
Brask
VIII *LINT-READER* 145
Szanto
LOVE AND GROCERIES 157
Brask

We had collaborated on other projects, never on short stories. We find working together forces us to consider, then reconsider. This time we began by agreeing on six arbitrarily chosen elements: a diary, brothers, April, and so on. We each wrote a story in which these six elements played a significant role. From the resulting two stories we chose six new elements, three from each: specifically, I chose two elements from his story, one I selected from my own. And from those stories, six new elements. And so on.

I

SENSE

GEORGE SZANTO

SUICIDE NOTE

PER BRASK

SENSE

GEORGE SZANTO

"Bloody murder! Bloody hell!"

Not Charlie's usual kind of language. But fair enough, right then. Weeks and weeks of this kind of thing could lead you to anything, from howling incantations to smashing out physically. Charlie had just put the TV on, right? and already he was screaming at what was coming through.

The game's against Pittsburgh, it's the ninth and we've got the tying run on third and the go-ahead's on second and nobody's out and Peppereeno's pinch-hitting and he smashes a screaming liner to left and this Pirate third baseman leaps it must've been four feet up and three sideways and damn but he catches the ball and doubles us off third and throws to their shortstop, it's a goddamn triple play and the game's over and Vancouver loses again!

All right, so sometimes the breaks go with us and sometimes against; the team, I mean. But, Charlie claimed, they *always* went against when he flicked a game on, or even only caught it like on the car radio. He swore he hadn't seen or heard us victorious since he became a fan again six weeks after we'd started winning like crazy back in May when Lefty Lowell took over the managing. Charlie said he can tune in to the game in the seventh and we're ahead 10-1, and the Cougars blow it right there, and we lose something like 13-10. I mean, he'd got so paranoid he said it was him that jinxed us. I told him, "Listen, don't talk like that with any other media guy around or he'll do some human interest story on you and there'll be a thousand law-abiding citizens ready to hang you by the privates." I mean, what can you say except, Sure is a strange coincidence. I started watching a bunch of games with Charlie and damned if it didn't happen every time—either we were losing anyway and we just couldn't catch up like we used to, or they'd come roaring from behind. When Charlie listened to a game from the start, well the national anthem was about as good as we got.

And hell, when he didn't listen in, we were golden. It was truly strange.

See, I'm the one turned him back into a fan—he used to be, years ago. But he had this kid brother who played, he loved the kid but they had a kind of falling out and baseball went with it. So sometimes I blamed myself for the whole mess. Except Charlie and me've been best friends for years and if I hadn't turned him on to the game again, well somebody else would've. I mean, the whole city had the fever.

But this thing that happened when he tuned in sure was weird.

Lefty thought it was pretty weird too. On the 4th of July they'd been in first place, twenty-two games up on the Dodgers in second. Two of his pitchers, Bertrand and Michaels, were on their way to a thirty win season for sure, and four of his regulars were voted National League All-Stars. The Vancouver Cougars, a fifth year expansion team (first four in last place), were the darlings of thousands of old and millions of new fans from Winnipeg and Edmonton down to Denver and across to Portland and even Seattle. In Vancouver itself the Cougars were titans, heroes of the sort that give meaning and hope to life, the kind of men that turn shared experience into daily joy and passing reality into myth and majesty. And Lefty Lowell, the most extraordinary managerial phenomenon in all baseball, possibly all baseball history, was a colossus among giants, king of the gods. (If you happened to be a Padres or an Expos fan, of course, you hated him and called him dumb lucky; or, for those who believe in such things, he'd sold his soul.) "I don't get it, Harry," Lefty muttered. Again, again.

Harry, who was usually at Lefty's side—some said he was half of Lefty's brain, others said his bodyguard—took the last piece of pizza.

"It was golden. Now it's like we've been, I don't know, spooked. Know what I mean?" This was maybe the millionth time in the last month this thought passed through Lefty's mind, probably the hundredth since he'd first spoken it out loud a week ago; mostly to Harry.

"Yep." Harry sipped his beer.

"I mean, each single day I'm still figuring it right. But there comes this moment, every time we're about to blow it, when I see it, I *watch* it go out of control. Know what I mean?"

"Yep."

"I mean, from twenty-two up down to a goddamn piddling three game lead and three weeks to go—cripe, I don't know."

Harry took a gulp of air and emptied his beer stein. He couldn't breathe and drink at the same time because he'd been a middleweight, a contender once, who quit after his nose got irredeemably flat but before his brains got scrambled (also he'd done nine years for armed robbery, caught when he was shot in the leg so he walks with a limp). Most important, he was Lefty Lowell's lucky charm, not to mention best friend. He'd do anything for Lefty. He said, "It's against nature. Right now this losing. And before, all that winning too. It's against nature, Lefty." Like he'd said a dozen times.

"And I'll tell you, nature's a whole lot bigger'n you or me know." For that moment Lefty looked back over the years. Then they had another couple of beers and couldn't for the life of them work out why things went wrong.

Because Lefty'd figured it all so right, years back, back in the beginning. He'd gone out to Dobie, Wyoming, unattached—"yeah, a real bad divorce, real stinker"—and got a job at the Coke bottling plant there. One spring morning he read in the Dobie *Dispatch* where the Rotarians were looking for managers for a couple of Little League teams. He'd gone over and the Rotary sports committee guy turned out to be so desperate he gave Lefty the Tastee-Freeze Tigers. Well he worked the devil out of those kids and taught them to use *all* their natural talents and they won the Dobie Championship and lost out only in the semifinals, state-wide. The second year he got his Tigers all the way to the Little League World Series, and in Honolulu the Tigers beat the Kyoto Red Sox—the Japanese boys were over-disciplined, nearly military—and for a week it put Dobie on the map. It also got Lefty five job offers from the pros, two to manage and three to coach. He opted for a coaching job with the Median Athletics in Class A, a perennial loser bought by the Cougar organization when Vancouver got its franchise. The A's fired the manager after losing the first ten games of the season, and Lefty Lowell took over; the team said they trusted him. Median, New Hampshire, wasn't much of a baseball town till Lefty arrived and it hasn't done much since, but for that season there wasn't anybody in New Hampshire between three and a hundred-three who wouldn't swear Lefty Lowell was as close to a god as anybody they'd ever get to know about; he took the Athletics right to the Class A pennant. Next spring, after the Cougars lost sixteen of their first nineteen, they brought Lefty in and the winning streaks began.

At first Lefty explained it by saying he understood the game from the inside: you see your players' strengths and weaknesses and you work them. Then he said he knew how to psych out the opposition, he had great scouts' reports and knew how to read them. (Except every baseball writer knows the Cougars have the world's lousiest scouting system.) Once in July he was being interviewed (needled, he said afterward) and he blew up, right in front of the camera: "How many senses you got? Any sense at all?" The sportscaster said, "Uh, five." "Well," said Lefty, "I got thirteen. And number eight tells you to (bleep) off."

Whatever so-called explanation he gave, it wasn't ever near enough to account for his uncanny ability to, for example, shuffle the batting order day after day, just a bit sometimes, sometimes radically, using all fifteen fielders, some on and some off, bunching those players who'd get the hits that day, sending in just the right pinch-hitter or pinch-runner. It was as if he knew, an hour before the game, who was going to get on when. Truly uncanny. (The reporter who did baseball on Channel 7, the one Lefty blasted, had once called it hunch-power, and the label stuck.) Or for a different example, just how long to leave a pitcher in. If, say, Doug Bertrand, 19-2 by the end of July, walked two in, say the eighth, sometimes Lefty stayed with him, sometimes he brought in Viv Smith or Randy McDougall who had sixty-seven saves between them; whichever choice, Lefty was dead on.

Not that the Cougars won all their games for Lefty. But by July 4 they were 58-21, which meant they'd lost five since he moved in.

About the end of July, Charlie (called Red by most everybody except me; and his ex who always said Charles, which gives you an idea why they split up) Lachine was one of the millions to get hooked on the Cougars. Back in his early twenties he'd been a fan when his younger brother Tommy'd pitched. But their pa had been so against Tommy playing, Charlie couldn't ever let on he went to games or even read the sports news. The old man, an engineer, wanted both Charlie (he wasn't called Red till his late twenties when he let his beard grow and it came in brass red) and Tommy both to come into the engineering plant he, Lachine senior, had built out of nothing: go to school and get the training and join him. The old man figured that was how he'd fulfill his part of the promise they'd all made to Ann, the kids' mum, just before she died at thirty-seven (she and Lachine never had time to enjoy his success, he was in the plant maybe sixteen hours a day, 360 days a year)—the three of them should always stay close, really together. So the kids, they were seven and eleven then, had to do everything the old man said, for the sake of their mum. This was okay by Charlie, more or less. But it didn't wash for Tom. He played a lot of ball starting around ten, he was a good pitcher; he didn't study any too hard and then he messed around with drugs there at school, a little pot first, and later hash, and when he went up to semi-pro ball he was using peyote and LSD—not while playing, he wasn't into that, but after a game, or the days between assignments. That was the time Charlie was a baseball fan, staying close to Tom on account of what their mum'd wanted for the family; it wasn't hard, he liked the kid. And they went trout fishing together. Those were the best times ever. Once the old man went with them and he spent the whole day arguing with Tommy; they didn't invite him along after that. And baseball? The old man stayed so down on it, if Charlie went to a game there had to be a lie.

Later when they were together Charlie'd argue with Tommy too. "You don't want to do engineering, okay at least do some course in goddamn business law. We need a lot of legal help."

But for Tommy the plant was too boring and obvious. When he was pitching, he said, he didn't know what was going to happen next; always new possibilities, depending on how much control he had, how good the next batter was, and the next. He'd developed this pitch, it was unique, spooky, that he called "the timeball." It seemed to slow down sometimes, or sometimes speed up, halfway to the plate. He couldn't explain it, he could just throw it. Control it, he used to say to Charlie, just by sort of thinking at it. And nobody could hit it. It made his adrenaline flow like crazy—every time he was on the mound it was a kind of danger: get it over so slow nobody can touch it, or whip it in for the last twenty feet; is it going to do it this time? Pitching like that led him to playing around with mushrooms, too. Tommy wanted what he called "something different," all the strange unexpected things out there, right now, simultaneous, except nobody can see them; or stuff that'd happen differently in the future. Naturally he wouldn't listen to Charlie.

Finally Tom and the old man quit even arguing; the old man said Charlie'd best forget about his brother; Charlie told his pa where to get off; later they made up again; at last it stopped being an issue because for the season Tom was out of town so much they rarely saw each other. Then it came to a head when Tom was called up by the Cards for spring training; he'd been voted best southpaw in AAA-ball the fall before and he was ready. On the first day of the season, in Philly, Tom was arrested for selling an ounce of peyote to an agent who, Tom's lawyer argued at the trial, entrapped him.

Except, Tom explained to Charlie, he had to deal, he'd been in debt to a couple of guys, and now just when he was near even this had to happen; he had a wad stashed but the narc brought him in before he could pay them off. So on top of everything these two guys were really pissed.

The judge gave him eight years: an example to young athletes everywhere. (Some said this judge, who accepts season tickets to the Phils every year for his work with Suburban Youth, just didn't want a kid like Tom in the St. Louis organization.) Tom didn't appeal.

The whole thing killed the old man. In the old days you'd've called it a broken heart. Technically it was a flu he didn't fight that turned into pneumonia he did nothing about. Tom spent three and a half years in jail, never answered Charlie's letters, Charlie stopped writing. Tom got paroled out and Charlie'd lost track of him. Which was why from the time the old man died till the beginning of July, Charlie had given up on baseball.

I was at Julius's Bar and Grill having a couple of beers with Harry one night after I'd filed my story for the late news. I'd known Harry since he came into town with Lefty back in May, he was one of my best sources; except sometimes he gave me the creeps. We'd won, 6-2. I happened to know Charlie was up in the Cariboo doing some fly fishing, which is the thing he likes best in the world, no exceptions. Maybe it was the third beer that loosened me up, maybe a real concern for the team; who knows. Anyway I told Harry about this crazy coincidence, that there was this guy I knew who thought it was maybe his fault the Cougars were losing, it was like he zapped 'em by turning on the radio or the TV. Well Harry went all cold and staring like he'd turned to stone and he asked me who was this guy. All of a sudden I felt like I'd said too much, except I didn't exactly know too much what, I mean it was only a weird sort of coincidence; so I pulled back, I said, "All I know is everybody calls him Red."

"You don't know his name and he's your friend." Harry looked at me like I was a dead carp.

"We just sort of hang out together sometimes," I said, "he's just a guy who comes in here sometimes," and I was relieved when he dropped it.

Of course the next morning I got a call from Lefty, he all polite and saying how much he'd like to meet this Red, maybe Red could tell him something. I said Red's out of town, which was true. Lefty said when he's back maybe; and I made it sound like I'd see what I could do. We let it go at that.

Except when Charlie got back there was this problem: somebody'd broken into his place and they'd bashed in the screen of the colour television and the black and white'd been dropped down the stairs and his three radios were smithereened. Also there was a note: "Never tune in a Cougar game again, you want to look like your TV?" Oh for creepsake, I thought, Lefty wouldn't've— Lefty'd never believe a cockamamie story like— "Who've you told about this thing with the Cougars?"

Charlie went, "I don't know—half a dozen guys maybe."

So I felt a lot better. "Let it go, tell the insurance you've been vandalized and flush the note down the toilet."

The next day Charlie discovered they'd stolen his car radio. After he got back.

The Cougars began to win again, regularly. They took the division title by September 9, and ended the season nine games up on the Cards. In the east the Expos won it on the last day of the season, bashing the Mets 14-3; so we had the first all Canadian playoff series ever and for ten days everybody from Victoria to Goose Bay talked about nothing else. South of the border, to the surprise of sportscasters and politicians, Canada was seen as the suddenly gorgeous younger sister: not really noticed all these years, then there she was, grown up into a real live beautiful lady. The Red Sox-Angels series, quickly over when the Sox took it in four straight, interested nobody outside the metropolitan Boston or greater L.A. area.

The Cougars won the two games in Vancouver, the first a scoreless pitching duel into the bottom of the eleventh when Teeter tripled with one away and Lefty had a hunch and pinch ran nineteen-year-old Ricky Call who (after one pitch, a call strike) promptly stole home; Vancouver went delirious. The next day the Cougars won 8-5. In Montreal the Expos won the next two, 4-3 and 6-3; then the Cougars came back with a 2-1 beauty (all runs scored in the ninth), Bertrand getting his second win and McDougall coming in for the save. The sixth game, back in Vancouver, was over by the third inning, the Cougars scoring eight runs, five of them unearned; final score, 9-3.

Lefty Lowell was mighty pleased, mighty happy. The end was coming, he could nearly touch it. Heck, he could practically taste it.

Charlie Lachine was terrified but angry too, he told me. What the hell power is this, to make the Cougars lose? He'd been scared stiff since his place got messed up: what if Vancouver started losing without him listening in? How'd they ever know it wasn't his fault? The more he talked, the madder he got. He heard about the two losses in Montreal, and was terrified about just going out of the house, and panicked to his kidneys to stay home where they could find him. He said he felt like he stank from fear.

"Why don't you go fishing," I said.

And he blew up. Did I think he was a *complete* chickenshit? Or did I really believe he was some sort of magic weirdo who would really cause a goddamn major league goddamn baseball team to lose just by turning on the effing radio for cat's sake? Jesus Christ.

I tried to calm him, "It's all coincidence, come on take it easy, cool it out."

But he wasn't having any of it. He took a triple scotch to get the smell of himself, he said, out of his nostrils. Naturally it didn't work.

The World Series began in Boston. Earlier, in the eastern division race, Toronto had given Boston a real run for their money, it didn't end till the last week, and now a hundred million baseball fans south of the 49th parallel were retroactively relieved. The pretty little sister was one thing; her taking over the family would've been something else altogether.

Bertrand won the first game for the Cougars, 3-1, Lefty going with him all the way despite a trouble-filled seventh that ended with a bases loaded double play; but it was a three up and three down eighth and ninth. The second game was come-from-behind ball, Vancouver getting two in the seventh to win it 5-4; Smith had the save. Lefty felt pretty damn good.

Harry wasn't happy yet.

"You will be soon, pal," Lefty told him as they boarded the plane for Vancouver.

Later Red said to me he couldn't stand it any more, not listening, not knowing. On that Thursday afternoon he tuned in, "just for an inning," in the sixth. We blew a two run lead and lost, 7-4.

Lefty Lowell had watched his so-called hunch power drain from him in the top of the sixth. What he felt was this: till then it was as if he'd been able to look through the surface of the game, into its heart; suddenly everything went opaque, chalky. Till then the game pattern had been completely clear; suddenly the lines started running into each other, it was all a blur.

Harry watched them score five in the sixth from the box just over the dugout. He left early. The game ended, score unchanged, as he backed into Red Lachine's driveway. He pulled a ski mask over his head and took his pistol from the glove compartment. He limped around back, found the kitchen door open, and walked in. No sound, no radio or anything. He looked through the living room, dining room; nobody. He went upstairs. All rooms were empty; except the bathroom, which was locked. "Come out Mr. Lachine. I won't hurt you, but we have to talk." No movement, no sound. "I'd prefer not to break down the door, Mr. Lachine." Silence. "But I will if you don't come out. We have to reach an agreement."

Slowly the handle turned. Through the crack Red stared at the ski mask, panicked doubly, pushed at the door to slam it shut. But Harry got his shoe in the way. Red came out.

"Shall we go to the living room, Mr. Lachine."

"Oh. Sure."

Harry's limp was pronounced as he walked down the stairs; it sounded an off beat. In the hall Harry hit Red on the head with his pistol. Red went out, and down. Harry backed his car into the garage, tied Red's hands and feet, bound his eyes and bundled him into the trunk. He drove out the ferry, crossed the bay to a small summer house on the Sechelt Peninsula, lonely in the beginning of October. There he sat Red on a chair, tied him in place till he regained consciousness, fed him some soup and left.

Red had never been much of a hero but now he was furious—goddamn it nobody tied him to a chair in the middle of nowhere. Aloud he said to the room, "I'm getting out of this." Well he pulled and pushed and scraped skin off his arms till he was worn out and he fell asleep. Next day he slowed himself down, he was hungry and feeling weak; also he'd gone light-headed. Around mid-afternoon at last he got this idea, maybe he was tied to the chair but the chair wasn't tied to anything and it was wood so he rocked it back and forth, back and forth till it fell over and he was under it and knocked himself out. When he woke up it was dark and he figured he wasn't much better off than before but at least he could crawl, more like drag himself, over to a kind of railing, maybe a staircase, and he worked a leg in between a couple of rails. Well it took time, maybe an hour, maybe three, but he broke off one of the legs, then slowly slowly he swung around and wedged the back in between two railings and in the devil knows how long he'd got it loose and he was exhausted but he kept pushing, and finally damned if the thing didn't break off and the ropes slid out from under, loose enough now so he could work his wrists free and untie the chair's legs from his legs. It was getting light when he got out of the house—no food, nothing in the kitchen—and about noon before he'd worked his way down to the road and hitched a ride to the ferry.

At four p.m. I opened my door and it was Charlie. "I got a story for you," he said.

"A sports story?"

"Nope. Kidnapping."

"Then it's not my story."

Charlie said, "What's happened with the Series?"

"We won yesterday, but lost this afternoon."

Harry and Lefty heard it on the news: Red Lachine, prominent Vancouver engineer, was abducted at gunpoint two days ago from his West Point Grey home but managed to escape from his captors. He couldn't recognize the man because the guy was wearing a ski mask. He had no idea what the motive was.

"I got to kill him now, Lefty."

"Easy, Harry. Easy."

"I'm not gonna let him do this."

"Red Lachine."

"That's the guy."

"We could pay him a visit."

"What?"

"Me, anyway."

"Reason with him?"

"Maybe."

"What do you mean, maybe? Don't you remember anything?"

"Too much. I want to talk to him."

"Okay. And if it don't work—squeeze."

It had to be that evening; they were flying to Boston first thing tomorrow. Lefty called Red Lachine. Nobody home, of course.

I got a call from Harry about 11:30. Red was already asleep—I'd given him a couple of pills. "Can you locate Red tonight? Lefty's got to talk to him."

"Maybe I can, maybe I can't."

"Try."

I said I'd call back. I woke Red, not the easiest thing in the world, and we talked about it, and finally we agreed he ought to see Lefty, that'd solve it; maybe.

Lefty and Harry showed up around 1:00 a.m. Lefty came in, greeted me by apologizing for the blow-up back in July, I said forget it. Silence. Harry said maybe he'd stay at the door, let Lefty talk to Red alone. It was okay by me if he didn't join us. Me, I wouldn't've missed this for the world.

Well, Red came out from the kitchen still sort of groggy and walked over to Lefty. Red reached out his hand and Lefty took a second, then stuck out his. Red said "I really admire what you've done with the Cougars, Mr. Lowell."

"Yeah. Thanks. Thanks a lot."

They talked right to the point, about what Lefty'd heard from Harry about Red's weird sense of his ability, maybe for ten minutes. But all the time Lefty was real uncomfortable. Finally he got up like with a jump and ended by laughing sort of nervously and saying, "Well whatever it is, we only got to win one more and you could do us a favour by not listening to the game or watching, okay?" They went to the door together.

"Sure. I promise."

Lefty shook Red's hand. "Thanks." He went out.

Red watched Lefty and Harry walk away; and recognized the limp. Goddamn—!

Most of the way back they drove in silence. Finally Harry couldn't stand it. "Well?" More silence. "You want I should off him?"

From Lefty, only silence.

About quarter to seven, not the next morning but the morning after, my phone rang. I always panic when it goes off in the middle of the night, it usually means bad news; that's when my mother called when my father had his heart attack. I should've been in Boston for the last game, or games, but I stayed because Charlie was so completely panicked by Harry with the limp; and, I've got to say, me too. I picked up the phone. "Yeah?"

"Let me talk to Charlie Lachine."

"Who?"

"Charlie. Your friend Red."

"He doesn't live here. Look, who is—"

"Tell him it's his brother. Tom."

"Yeah?"

"Yeah."

So I woke Red and told him; he didn't believe me; I said, "Talk to the guy, for creepsake."

So he picked up the phone and he listened for a couple of minutes and he hung up.

"Well?"

"He says he called from Boston. He says he's heard about me on the radio, what I can do to the Cougars. He says come to Boston this afternoon, there's a plane ticket at the airport and a reservation at the Hotel Cabot and he's got two tickets for tomorrow's game."

"And?"

"And he'll meet me in my hotel room tonight at 10:00."

"So?"

"It's incredible."

"You believe him?"

"I don't know."

The Cougars lost that afternoon, 4-1; all fair and square. Lefty saw the game pattern clearly, grouped the strengths, tried his darndest, but nothing worked. The Sox were simply damn good, too good.

Three-all for the series; tomorrow would tell everything.

Charlie's room was a suite. All paid for. Well whatever Tommy'd been doing he must've been doing it right. I walked over to my hotel, a cheapie at the far end of the Common.

Charlie was just a hint completely terrified at being in Boston. What if he heard a piece of the game on any chance radio? Oh yeah, the same kind of thing might've happened in Vancouver, but there at least he knew the environment.

He also knew he was really pleased his brother had called; he'd sort of suddenly rediscovered he cared a lot for the kid, he told me on the flight across. He figured he'd stopped blaming Tommy for the old man's death long ago, he just tried not to think about it. I'd never seen him so excited. "Imagine," he said, "flying three thousand miles on the strength of a phone call." Till he got to the airport he hadn't really believed there'd even be a ticket. He said he thought he recognized Tom's voice. He could've called the airline before leaving, just to check, but he decided to take the risk and he shared a cab with me.

There was a knock on Red's door.

Lefty Lowell came in. "Hiya Charlie."

"Lefty? What the hell?"

"It's me. Tom."

"Look—"

"Plastic surgery. Changed my name. But I couldn't hide, not finally."

"For cat's sake, Lefty—"

It took Lefty/Tom maybe half an hour to convince Charlie: private details about their mother, the bear that attacked when they were fishing once, an old friend of Tom's that Charlie'd loaned two Gs to to cover poker mistakes—all the kind of information you don't research just for a joke.

So naturally Charlie was stunned. He came back slow. "Why? What the hell d'you disappear for? Listen, you want a drink? I need one." He poured them both a scotch and wondered if Lefty/Tom wouldn't prefer some dope; or whatever.

" 'Cause they were after me, Charlie—these guys I owed. I had twenty-nine thousand stashed away. The only thing I had to show for three-plus years in jail. Not even six thou a year. But it was a stake. So I got rid of my face."

"And you didn't let me know?"

"You didn't come to see me in three years, Charlie."

"You didn't exactly answer my letters."

"And what was I supposed to say? You were out there. You could've dropped by."

Charlie said quietly, "Something just—sort of kept me away."

"Yeah."

"Know what I mean?"

"His ghost."

"Come on."

"It's hovering. All the time."

"What d'you mean?"

"What you're doing against the Cougars."

"You don't believe—"

There was a long silence then. Charlie was just thinking and thinking, all the thoughts disconnected at first; then slowly pieces started to pull together. Suddenly there was only one piece extra. "Tom? Why'd you call?"

Tom was sitting there, sipping scotch, waiting for the question. " 'Cause I wanted you here."

"What for?"

"After I met you—after *Lefty* met you?—I saw how the pattern worked."

"Yeah?"

"Where all of it, you and me and baseball, all fit in."

"And the old man?"

"Him, his ghost. At least its representative."

"Me?"

"Yep."

"You don't need me for that."

"Wrong."

"Why?"

"You got to ask?" Tom finished his scotch.

"You could tell me."

" 'Cause I love you, you ass."

That stopped Charlie short. Not 'cause he hadn't known what Tommy'd say. Because he had.

It was the end of the serious talk. Tom/Lefty had to be at Fenway early. Except Tom made it clear Charlie had to be at the game too.

"You're out of your tree. I'm renting a rowboat from one to four and sitting in the middle of the river."

"I want you *there.* Away from the TV and the radio. You, personally."

"Yeah?"

"Yeah."

Whatever happened in the last game, they'd get together after. Back in Vancouver.

Later that fall Tom and Charlie Lachine bought, jointly, a fishing camp in the Chilcotins. Charlie'd sold off the plant, which he figured was half Tommy's anyway. (They argued about that till Tom figured if a piece of the cash went into the camp he wouldn't mind sharing that with Charlie.)

Lefty Lowell quit baseball, he just disappeared one day back into the same silence he'd come out of. As he told the reporters after the last game, "I figure I've done just about everything now." His new face in January was halfway between the young Tom and the recent Lefty.

The next summer, at Kamp Ketchelotte, they had two regular guests, just as they've had every since: a guy whose game leg makes it clumsy stepping down into the boat; and a sportscaster from Vancouver.

And how could Lefty see the heartbeat of a game? And how did Charlie undermine the drive? And why do ghosts grasp tight to memories? And who won the Vancouver-Boston World Series? Can such things really happen in the world? One day perhaps we'll learn the rules for solving problems much like these; maybe that day we'll all be Cougar fans.

Meanwhile I'll write about those things we still don't understand: ask questions, probe about, sometimes bring together brothers long divided—

SUICIDE NOTE

PER BRASK

Winnipeg, April 26, 1985

TO: Bjarne Hviid
187 Østerbrogade
DK 2100 Copenhagen Ø
Denmark

Dear Bjarne,

When you read this letter I will be dead, I'm happy to say. I'm addressing this to you because I think you're the one in the family best able to handle it.

When we met three weeks ago at father's funeral after so many years I nearly failed to recognize you. Your belly, your grey hair and your round face fooled me, even though we look very much alike. Imagine that it should take father's heart attack to reunite the family. What a reunion! Everyone seemed more concerned about meeting, or rather re-meeting, people they hadn't seen in ages than they were about father's death. I found it quite unforgivable, though, that Aunt Maren forced mother to stay up all night before the funeral to talk about "the old days" while getting herself into such a stupor she could barely stand at the graveside the next morning. I suppose that's what can happen when half the family lives in Denmark and the other half over here spread out over five thousand miles.

I am happy, though, that mother decided to bring father home to have the funeral in Ribe. He was, after all, a kind of "born-again" Dane. So he had to be buried in his *hjemby-hjemstavn* or whatever they call it—place of origin, I suppose, would be the bureaucratic translation for it.

That was when I made up my mind. During the festivities connected with father's funeral I decided to commit suicide. Not in depression over father's death. You know I was never close to him. In fact you probably saw more of him than I did. He would fly over Winnipeg on his way to Denmark each summer.

Never once did he stop over to visit. I would see him and mother maybe once every two or three years when business took me to Vancouver. You got three to four weeks of them each summer in Denmark. Don't misunderstand me, I don't envy you. I'm quite happy never to have seen much of any of you. Not that I don't love you. I do. In my own curiously remote way, I enjoy our relationship better in my memory than in actuality. During the funeral this became crystal clear to me. It was an awkward time for me. People made fun of my accent and would simply not believe that speaking Danish has become quite a task. I don't know how this happened but over the years I stopped thinking in Danish and began to think in English so that I now have to translate from English into Danish when I speak, which naturally produces an accent. I'm sure you've noticed in my birthday cards and letters that writing in Danish has become an absolute impossibility for me. So please find it in your heart to accept this note in English. I would not be able to say what I really want to say in broken Danish.

Seeing Denmark in her "spring clothes" in early April with all the beautiful flowers, *Erantis*, *Krokus*, *Påskelilje*, did in fact make me melancholy. I'm convinced that the ever-changing weather affects people that way. Seen from inside those continually changing weather patterns, life itself looks unruly and uncontrollable, every intention defeated as it is barely brought into the world. Nothing lasts.

When I first came to Canada I found it a very difficult and strange place. People were very nice—too nice at times. Canadians want only to produce niceness around themselves. All conflicts must be mediated—"surely, we can deal with this as reasonable adults. Give and take. Compromise." For a Dane, who grew up in a country where pursuit of the ultimate meaning of life in all its angst-ridden implications is the first duty of each citizen, the Canadian cultural foundation seems somewhat odd. It certainly seemed odd to me when I arrived. People appeared to me to be willing to contradict themselves all the time or to hold several opinions on any subject in order to make the compromise necessary to establish a relationship. Here a relationship is the by-product of your negotiations with others. The Canadian protects himself. And, so, it is almost impossible to belong here.

Oh, after several years you begin to have the feeling of belonging. For me it took at least eight to ten years to feel that "this is *my* country." A very peculiar feeling to develop. Nationalism is simple enough to understand when you are talking about where you grew up, learnt to walk and talk or loved someone for the first time. It is quite a different matter to develop such emotions towards a place you moved to as an adult. Still, I started to feel a certain union with this place. Canadians have a hard time accepting that. As a professor of Canadian literature I attend conferences each year. At these conferences I am often told that my feelings for Canada are false because I will never really be able to understand the essence of Canadian culture or the psyche it has produced. For that one must be born and bred here.

I remember one particular conference in Toronto in the mid-70s where after a session on, I forget exactly what, I was having a couple of beers with some colleagues. They were contemporaries of mine. We sat around a table in a smoke-filled tavern. All seven (I think) of us were dressed in jeans and wore corduroy, or tweed, jackets. As the evening wore on the conversation became looser and the discussion moved towards "Canadianness" in art. What makes a Canadian novel Canadian, a Canadian short story, a Canadian play, that sort of thing. During the conversation I suggested that the very pursuit of "Canadianness" might be dangerous and limiting to people's free pursuit of reactions to their environment, their background, whatever. That in fact a country like Canada with her history and the varied heritages of her people, the question of a homogeneous, Canadian "identity" might be the expression of the old WASP elites' will to hegemony over "the ethnics," a final attempt to stave off the death of "the good old days."

This suggestion was by no means taken lightly. After a few polite counter-suggestions, a member of the group told me that I might as well go back to where I came from. When I protested that I as a Canadian citizen had as much right as any to voice my opinion on the issues of my country I was met by laughter. I'm sure this sounds some historical bells for you. So certainly in those circles two classes (maybe more) of citizens exist. Many of these ardent Canadians, of course, have living grandparents who came here from elsewhere—I wonder which class they belong to. It would be easy enough to reject such statements at conferences with a sleight of hand if one didn't run into this kind of attitude so often.

As a newly arrived immigrant, one is considered interesting, at times even cute, and at the best of times a challenging foreigner. This doesn't last long, however. After a few years as a "landed immigrant" you are encouraged to become a citizen. People teaching at universities, who are still landed immigrants after ten to fifteen years are met with suspicion. Perhaps rightly, but for the person facing the choice, it is not always easy to let go of the notion that you might return to where you came from. I don't think that necessarily makes you any less useful here, as long as your work is good.

Time and your new relationships do combine, however, to make you feel at home neither here nor where you came from. I had a curious experience visiting Denmark about seven years after I'd left. I was in a bookstore looking at new Danish literature but I couldn't choose any books. I felt without a frame of reference, a context through which I could relate to these new authors. I had to read either all the new books or none. I simply did not have the energy to read seven years of literature in order to ferret out the development of "my" culture since I left. When I returned I applied for Canadian citizenship, not as a rejection of Denmark, but in acknowledgement that its current life was not part of me, though its history was, and with that history I could still participate as a full member of Canadian life. Changing your citizenship does not express anything but a psychological commitment to stay and live with the possibilities of your new country.

Still, even if you have progressed through these stages it is no guarantee that you will be accepted by other Canadians for what you now are—a Canadian. Some will not let you be what you have become—one of them. In other words, they will not let you belong and as a consequence you don't.

My need to belong is strong, Bjarne.

When I saw you three weeks ago I felt like a character in a Greek tragedy seeking some physical sign, a scar, which would identify you as one of my kin. But these powerful emotions described so well in those ancient tragedies are certainly quite foreign to you and me. We have no *Oikos* to protect and further. I have some good memories which I treasure as I treasure good films. It wouldn't really have mattered whether you were or were not my brother. We have both changed so much in the past twenty years that we are complete strangers.

You were surprised by my singleness several times during my stay. First, I think, out of staid concern for my sexual orientation. But Bjarne, the matter is really quite simple. I have not been able to develop a relationship with a woman which was gratifying for both of us for more than six or seven months. This may well be the result of some psychological deficiency of mine but I nonetheless think that I share this inability with a great many people—many of them married. My abilities to bond, to nurture a long-lasting relationship may be few but I am, at least, honest. I find the pursuit of oneness with others pathological, in fact. This pursuit of oneness is an expression of the infantilism our culture encourages. We want to feel safe in the world. Naturally, we want the world to be one with us, we want to avoid making the distinction between ourselves and the world and so we create fictions of history, nations, and families which will suppress our desperate instinctive sense of randomness and unbridgeable separation.

I think we can visit each other's worlds from time to time but ultimately I do not think that we can build workable worlds together which do not involve some kind of tyranny.

To invite you to visit my world at your leisure I've sent my diary along with this letter. It is perhaps a little sad that we cannot share the thoughts written in our diaries while we live but a diary is destroyed if it is intended for immediate broadcast. I don't want you to feel obligated to read it. If it makes you feel uncomfortable, throw it away. I have not written in it for about six months, so even I feel distant from my latest entries. It has become, for me, a historical document like the memories I have of our childhood.

I have only one request to make of you with regards to my funeral. Please make certain that I will not be buried in Canada nor in Denmark. If you can manage it I would much prefer my ashes to be spread over the ocean. I do not want any signs on earth of my existence. I do not intend melodrama with this request, I wish only my existential destiny.

Well, I have troubled you enough and I thank you for your patience while reading this letter.

Med de kærligste hilsner fra Hans-Henrik

II

ON CHEEMY POND

GEORGE SZANTO

THE MOON

PER BRASK

ON CHEEMY POND *

A PREVIOUSLY UNWRITTEN EPIC BY ARISTOCRATES, FOUND IN AND DONE OUT OF THE ATTIC, TRANSFORMED TO UNRHYMED PROSAICS AT THE TIME OF CHEEMY POND

GEORGE SZANTO

Of glorious Athens from eons lost I sing, of Athens and its brace of royal mountains, of Athens loved by meddling Paris, treasured too by bounteous Pallas of the code-giving womb. Yea I sing of Athens wherein dwells the fair Cravemptor, victim of history unordained, stepdaughter of true doughty Menepossenon.

The lithesome Cravemptor, along her waving hair a stream of laurel, a mighty river sparkling 'cross her brow, she with breasts like maple honey, Cravemptor called The Sweet, La Belle, and Melancholy. She, Cravemptor, island from the pleasures heir to maidens striving for the status special to adulthood, mounting Athenian passions taught by Aphrodite passing in the night by woman's ear, whisp'ring strange and natural fancies to enrichen chaste Cravemptor's blush, plots to ply her ethnolithic soul in search of mettle firmer far than shades of pure and silent nights.

I would sing to you of causes for this longstanding dark affair. From old there burns the War of Spartan Federation, the angry decades filled with fire since peace has held its sway in Athens, generations grown to manhood swinging vain and alien swords in flickering defence of needs primeval, of rights long broken: to speak the daily Attic of their ancestors. And newly wrought, the false accord proclaimed at Cheemy Pond, the loss of right for distant citizens to parlay also in their many Attic tongues—Aieee! what perfidy was sung at Cheemy, what blithe and spurious explication—

But list! now stands before my mind and eye she who with her restless passion speaks of truths forgotten long by Athens's bravest

---

**Ed. note:* At the conclusion you'll find an interpretation to fit our times. For the pleasure of the epic, read the whole text first. For more immediate gratification, turn to p. 34.

men, by Athens's finest bards. She, Cravemptor, cries: "I anxiously display my swelling heart to you. Is time not rife for happiness to dwell once more in Athens's breast? Has not the hour been broached, have not our fortunes flared? We must ameliorate the state of our beleaguered citizens! And lest you feel I'm the self-mart'ring sort, hear carefully these words so you may learn the sensual ardours due to me."

Her cheeks that flush, her white and sky-blue tunic's velvet fall, her slender ankle's inward curve: these pictures fleet before me in the dithyrambs I sing. Such countless seasons since, yet stands she sharp before my eye. I see her smile a discontented arching hope and fantasize she can transport her Athens to a more than manly state. She now confides: "My heart pounds in my breast. I cannot find the heavy cork to dam the flow of my hot blood, nor stem the tide of undirected joy I find in this my canny tongue. For Athenkind and me, what anguish! I cannot raise a cunning lad deserving of my heart, no haughty blade submitting to my breast and all the joy wherewith he thereupon could lie and whereon prove his point."

Then Cravemptor's worth speaks the pictures her tongue cannot entwine. In later times her words might ring of self-sufficient woman's lot, her chant invincible in her heart. Yet here she lies upon a couch, a vision of despair for mortals yet unborn, a cool divisive space 'twixt her and he that sings her tale. But suddenly this silence is the solace she refuses.

"Athenian heroes are," she threnodizes, "a sordid lot. The young ones seek their wealth as Zeus-aspiring clerks in fett'ring stocks and well-chipped bonds, they strive to trade in freedom unaware 'tis this their very freedom that they trade, they lose momentum, die long before their central swords are tested. In future times, why I might join them if I could, but now— The old johns long since baptized in the fray, they've shot their thrust in battle and in camp, they've bolted from behind so many new recruits they've lost their sense of direction. Nor," an afterthought, "can they hope for glorious erection of statues to spurious lost youth."

How puissant sad rings out Cravemptor's song! It carries her to our own time, the tune unstoppable— What more than nothing can be left in this her dying world? The old men deeply scarred below the skin, the young return besieged by mortgaged dreams of wealth. So seek she must, she knows, a man with courage to admit his blatant cowardice. How few such blades in Greece!

One, abundant luck for her, she knows presumptive well: her own deep-wizened stepfather, a true dolorous elder statesman. "Or else I might never've survived," she allows.

Of her sovereign tongue I sing, it wets her lips which glisten as she cries, "And what would I, unborn, have done with my deep pining surge for love?" Allied queries fade to silence till, her right leg listless curving from the couch, she speaks the words of her dread tutor, Pallas Athena: "This problem has a vexing civil side: a base disaster how few children are newborn, the age-old Attic-speaking population soon may die away. Nor can they count on the gods or the priests for surprises, not as in grand times of yore. Or else I too might royal 'lympus mount, be gatten by imperial Zeus, unite with him in his two score and ten unequal states of grace."

I sing as well of the stout-legged maidservant, she who bears a golden harmonica as she steps swiftly from behind the stoa.

Cravemptor chants of Zeusian might; first-handled knowledge has she none. Her dirge pours forth: How foolish to assume that 'neath their royal mountain her city-state might futile independence find from yokes of falsely drawn desire. She fears this easy answer to the depths of her despair, it bodes yet unborn eons more of unrewarded wars. She needs, her ultimate resort, a coward like her lustrous stepfather.

Of the verse which ends in unhappy chorale I sing, as Cravemptor emotes her trepidation to the auriferous strains of the mournful harmonica.

Strophe: What's a maiden to do with her lust as she seeks a personal love, if her trust is just but induces no thrust from the blades yet elusive above!

Antistrophe: What's a lady to do with her sighs, her concupiscential dreams, when statusful cries bring fears to her eyes, her life cursing away till she screams:

Synstrophe: "What's a woman to do with her charms when her sighs are surprised with desire, and she calls in alarm for a man in her arms, for some blade to invade her with fire."

I weep as I croon of her cries for I know she sings true! Won't romance find a chance to enhance her anew?

From the depths of his late afternoon arrives her stepfather Menepossenon, a scarlet rose glowing 'gainst his flowing robes: thanatistic pomp befitting this aristocrat. He has laboured long to raise the Attic and the Spartan tongues to equal rectitude in each our houses, to leave them coexist in the twelve great city-states. Despite his interventions tireless and tiresome have these weakened states yet quarrelled on, and unreforged remain their fates, Ares's captains fast in place amidst quiescent citizens. Menepossenon, elsewise staunch and of patrician mien, caring not a morsel for the wares of our democracy, this Menepossenon in present days of darkness re-views himself a leader in the state, no candidate for chorus duty he: a leader still since so few others dare come forth. I sing of Menepossenon, yea even he, dispirited, phlegmatic now. Slow he chants the words of Manges, he who taught blind Homer: "All pulls apart. The middle is a mess. The cries of these sad days we may address to ourselves only. The end shall come. I, Menepossenon, of voice grow dumb. I may not speak felt words, but only what I ought. The Cheemy Pond accord will bring our state to naught. We old men know our truths, the young accept their lies. They'll never live so long, nor ever be so wise. Yet what good does our wisdom do if we're but ashes when we're through?"

Of Menepossenon in tears I sing, he sees pale before him the anguished Cravemptor, her status in his eye full equal to his love for all his adolescent kin—though sometimes some are more beloved, some less—she, Cravemptor of the roundling hips, the ever-wanting womb, the river sparkling brow, the special smile she saves for him. He wipes his eyes, his brow, slowly in his toga's folds, the red, the white. He cinches tight the withered cord about his waist.

Cravemptor speaks. "I overheard you, Father, reviling life. Your phrases I reject. There you stand, your memories filled rich with satisfying well-drained memories. You debated sharply then, the forum's own iconoclast, its great contender once, and gatted well if sometimes less than wisely in the shaded glens and private bedrooms of the city. Would our youth stray dangerous far were they to pattern, on your own, their lives?"

"No no Cravemptor," intones Menepossenon, sweet despair a-slaking at his voice, caring not a whit for popular convention. "I acted all too rarely out of abject fear. With full cowardice I could have united all twelve tribes. Too late, too late. Now death, the necessary end, stalks everywhere my pride. The youthful juices dry away. Nothing remains. All about me, nothing."

"Indeed, Stepfather," lilts the honour-bound Cravemptor, she of the manfully unbroken vestal, "nothing. But the mere nothings I search for are different from the nothings you possess. Indeed, there falls yet between your sighs that matter and that spirit similar true to the younger penduli I seek. For me alone there is surely—nothing."

"It is ever easy, Daughter," hoarsely whispers Menepossenon, "to find a slender Attic or a Spartic-speaking blade." He, yclept the Great Confederator, stares into the bitter distance, his wearied eyes already yearning for Elysium's fenceless fields.

Of Cravemptor's despair I sing as it seeks out Menepossenon

behind his sheet of silence: "Not when Athens drives them from me to their vulgar fiscal crusade."

These words cohere in Menepossenon's dark sagging heart: for she speaks true! Athens owes Cravemptor far far more than time has bought her. He speaks a father's agapistic promise, with all inversion fast intact: from then through time eternal this sanction lends its name to doing or to dying gladly, and humankind will call it the Vow of Menepossenon: "Cravemptor, daughter, storm-bred child, for you I'll find before I die a rapt'rous gat of vision wild. With him you anything can try."

Cravemptor, she whom women call The Fervent, throws her arms about her father's neck, applies a polyglottal kiss to his thin and grizzled jowl. Let no one now attempt to thwart her ethnocratic hopes! "Oh Daddy, yes I'll settle on anyone with mettle. The fact I'll have a gatter is the only joy that matters." Her moment overflows with doraded harmonic strains: "Here's what a woman must do with her concupiscential dreams— She shares her desires as her stepsire requires, 'cause he's dying to discharge her schemes." She leans her cheek 'gainst the rose on his chest.

I sing to you now of a turn in our epic, a specious sweep to the heart of the city. 'Tween narrow streets deep in the agora, midst mild meat pies and steaming pea-soup tureens, stands the stoa of prodigal Zeus himself, a glorious shed, its alabaster walls a-gleam 'gainst tearless skies, its brass roof glowing aquamarine. Here sits Croagulatias, arrived as if by parachute from the heavens themselves, Croagulatias known to our world as: Deus Ex Machina. When asked to explain his present terrain he is wont to disclaim: "The Deus Ex Machina I, at propitious moments appearing. You have no idea how I try to render my presence appealing."

He addresses the old women and men, the sparse and raggle-taggle children, remnants of the once proud population, those known to history as the Endlings. "Yes my good friends," oozes the monolithic Croagulatias, "I am an heroic spirit, the only justified man-god in Athens, and master of Cheemy Pond. My power is your power."

His delusion the Deus would make our illusion: a magician he may have been, a demigod to his maquinators only.

"In the end, await and see, I alone, I shall own the victory. This little plot, hatched today, by a father and a daughter, will fall my lot. Rely on me." He laughs and in a puff of smoke he vanishes, descending 'neath the shallow ground—this a parlour game achieved with gunpowder from China. No Endling in the city can fathom his tricks. Of China I sing in another epic.

To these Endlings few topoi remain. As they march about the centre of the city, they recite their attic slogans:

" 'The end stands grimly at hand' is a phrase we cannot withstand."

"Its sources we don't understand."

"Though we hear it throughout the land."

"It's an irreversible trend, so we pity ourselves."

"We depend on a pond in accordance with friends."

"We cannot defend it, much less amend it."

"Hence grimly we lend it our silent assent."

"As we bend our surrender to fend off contenders."

"And send off abstentions in face of the oncoming end."

The impotent few discourse chorically, their simple rhymes offered as a dying incarnation: thus it is when a people's battle ever chases words and signs and leaves the substance of a nation's heart and times to memory and foreign prattle. The Endlings would enlighten the meanest stranger of the baneful nature of the state. One, once a Senator, speaks to no one in particular. "We've seen all, we've known all. Therefore we dread all. We recognize a dire recipe when one is thrust before us: take one loverless amorous maiden, take one old man whose assets hang below the loosened cord around his waist. Consider these as history relates them. Recall conjunction, that eternal pact of nature. Do not ignore this fated liaison."

Some hear. Few think. None act. Though the subject is exhausted, the Endlings debate on.

I sing of Menepossenon guided by his stride toward his place in history. He falls upon their gabbling corner. They assail him with off-rhymes and surface couplets. He defends himself with vacuous codes of thrust and parry.

"Do not tamper with our laws," they cry.

Menepossenon, his cynic's laugh his armour, calls them all disabled cranks, bleakly swings his withered staff, cannot disperse their mangled ranks. At last he sits, grim weariness now sovereign in his bones, a silent stream of tears the only show of life. He cries aloud, "Abandon me incarnate here, you paradosic Endlings, and let my agony commence."

The Endlings, remisunderstanding, challenge him anew: "No agon can commence, you obfuscate the rule, without the presence of Endlings, you Athens-demeaning fool."

"Not I," shouts Menepossenon, warden of the shade, "but you.

Go on. Do what you must. You've ever lost our mortal trust."

The Endlings moralize. "You shouldn't bring yet greater danger to our city."

"You shouldn't destroy the few remaining balances, codes set by the gods themselves."

"It isn't nice."

"Restrain yourself, Menepossenon."

"What care I for the gods," moans the vengeful Menepossenon. "The gods have made our lot dependency, dependency on imperial Zeus, dependency on Croagulatias his tiny blinded despot, dependency on Cheemy Pond." The once-proud mien of Menepossenon decays. "Endlings, know that soon I die. Know my daughter goes unloved. The gods and you together have dismayed our codes. Regal Athens has tumbled the balance. Our state now binds Cravemptor in her grievous chastity."

"The love you would teach her can never find favour with Zeus. You've got to look elsewhere to get a good gat for a girl on the loose."

No, the Endlings do not understand. Never have they climbed the royal mountain.

"Is it wrong a father loves his daughter? If she cannot live in chosen love, then what use any code from up above?"

Cries out an ancient female Endling: "The codes must be, they reign supreme. And one day we will all redeem our souls before the throne of Zeus."

"While here our necks are in the noose? No thanks. I don't need your advice."

"We urge against your acts of vice," the Endlings squeal in unison.

Menepossenon fumes on. "Might as well, there's naught to lose."

Pants a little Endling, "We thought you had a state to lose."

Of Cravemptor now I sing, she of the red-brimmed eyes and tear-trimmed cheeks, Cravemptor seeking out her father down the city's darkling streets, beside bordellos boarded up, fearing should he chance to weaken, lest he lose his pithy vigour, waste it on a wayward wench. She has heard the little Endling's words and now pronounces, "Ah yes, the state may lose, but I would win, and happy should I be, were I but rid of it."

My lay is a lyric of actions, of moments long gone by. I dare not sing of meanings, nor would I like to try.

A toothless Endling speaks. "You must not sin at home, for the sake of our moral state!"

And Menepossenon responds, "Morality is merely private now. When each city, each village, prates ever as it will, the nation abdicates."

A well-dressed Endling harangues, his words by habit dictated: "The ship of state sails mightily. Moral law will never abdicate."

"The leaders of Athens have abdicated to Croagulatias," Menepossenon mourns.

"We shall have victory!" So screams an Endling bearing stocks upon his shoulders. Again he shouts this, and again. At last he has convinced himself.

"Now we must celebrate," calls Menepossenon, "for the end is at hand."

"The ship of state is in—" begins a mid-class Endling.

"As the ship founders, so let it sink." Thus concludes Menepossenon.

"Sink deep, sink deep," breathes the lusty Cravemptor. "Sink deep and we shall found a state."

With unfatherly hand, Menepossenon grasps one graceful elbow of the ethnoclast Cravemptor, looks into her red-trimmed eyes, proclaims his Vow shall be fulfilled: "The time has come for us to try. Daughter, know that soon I die. But 'ere that moment hear me cry: Yea, I'll go leaving a reason why."

I speak softly of desire as it layers the cracks of Cravemptor's soul. Her eyes tear-filled with happiness, she whispers, "Stepfather, dearest Father, I beg you 'ere you die, a daughter's arms, a daughter's charms, take you to satisfy."

Thus I sing of cornucopic intentions, of the love of a stepfather for a daughter, of the need of this stepdaughter for her father. Cravemptor and Menepossenon withdraw. In their wake, fear and awe.

The Endlings find no heart-felt rhymes. They hang their heads in fright and sorrow. Sorrow for what? They cannot say. They'll know tomorrow.

They do not note the dash of smoke, the flash of the risen Croagulatias. He of the thickened ectoderm lurks in the empty spaces of his mind and speaks under his breath, he his own best audience. "My hour is drawing nigh. I see with mine own eye the fools I've come to fry. I'll have them by and by."

At this moment of most profound conflict, know all of you how, as the fate of the royal mountain state lingers unresolved, the poet shall chant his voluntary parabasis. A strophe or two is common to these Attic festivities. Our need for such a moment now is strong, as Menepossenon and Cravemptor ply their parts in dusky glens beyond the focussed ears of this my song.

Above the regal skies blow winds of hurricano force! They rage and scream and cataract, and crack their cheeks and dry the sheets of Menepossenon's last virgin's bed!

The episodes of this, our passionate pretence, will not bring comfort to the city's habitants! The victory day of Zeus and Sparta comes anon, afore Cravemptor's sighs cease glist'ning in the sun! And her brow in the sullied torrent! Now we must make the best of such incontinence, and mediate our loss with couplets of defence:

So cracks a lofty state. Good night, good night. Although we lost we fought the noble fight—

But what could here be happier. Our parentheses is done. For Menepossenon returns, he grins, he knows he's won: "The ship of state may founder, but I was never sounder!"

And the comely Cravemptor, she of the ethnocopic womb, a-whispering, "Oh. Oh. Oh. Oh."

The Deus, again undisembodied, bowing lowly to the Endlings, clamours out his own refrain: "Did I not ably say the victory was mine, before I ever knew the nature of the crime? And if you think I'm getting ironicker then sing this to a mournful harmonica—"

And he chants a moritat of impossible hope, hope for Cravemptor, hope for Menepossenon, hope if not in this why then in future epics. In his song he is joined, for so it happened, by the Endlings of Athens. They extemporize a long-forgotten melody. The words belong to the Deus, the sense becomes as we hear it the song of the newborn city itself, those quatrains sung to this day in the terse translation of Thor-og Zegasen, and set in later years to lush harmonious strains—these now played on the city's own gilded harmonica as the chorale finale of the Tenth Symphony, called *The Unknown:*

"Tragic endings are avoided in distorted comedies. We request you listen closely for we only aimed to please. Athens made her soldiers bolters, bled her daughters' vital cores. Athens left her temples empty fighting puny Attic wars. Greece remains the patria nostra nowadays vicariously. 'Hear your children,' cries Cravemptor. 'Take their yearnings variously.'

"Be reminded we're but Endlings. Your diversion is our task. You're the readers, we're the traders, we say anything you ask. You've the money, you buy epics. You still fabricate your wars. All about you, emptied temples, ships of state become destroyers. We can't speak the way you ask us 'cause your payments tell us to. We're the mirror, you're the heroes— End of epic. Where are you?"

I sing once more of Attic thunder clashing, of Croagulatias's lightning as it blinds, of Endlings who skirmish in alleyways, who march with time-worn slogans thrust and lost above their hearts. Meneposssenon leers, Cravemptor moans, Zeus sweeps to dominion over the continent. I sing of it all.

Now hearken once again, return you to the title page, recall this modest timeless epic aspires not to allegory, and meditate upon our far-flung castings should these few lines reduced to modern drama be—

Athens, played by . . . . The official state of "Quebec"

Cravemptor, played by . . . . Montreal and its people, the thirty-plus ethnic groups of them

Menepossenon, played by. . . . . Pierre Elliott Trudeau

Sparta, played by . . . . Ontario

The Maidservant, played by . . . Jean Doré

Croagulatias, played by. . . . . . . Brian Mulroney

The Endlings, played by . . . . . . The Tories of Canada

Zeus, played by. . . . . George Bush

THE MOON

PER BRASK

Partially hidden behind two clouds sat the bright moon casting a shimmering line through the ocean, splitting it down the middle through the ruffled wavy surface into two separate worlds like the chambers of the human brain. On the beach, her toes in the water, she stood soaking in the night, communing with her moon in a language she didn't understand, a truly foreign language for which no translation existed but which was nonetheless exact in its visions and feelings. The scar running from the edge of her pubic hair around and over her hip and down the back of her left thigh was proof forever that the language she experienced on the beach, naked, in a state of communion at full moon was not merely an occurrence of the imagination. Dreams don't crack skulls or slash thighs.

A sixth sense activated her fear, the scar hurt, remembering. She broke out of her wakeful trance and ran down the beach around the bend and then into the dunes topped with sharp sheaths of grass. The moon followed, lighting her way, but also lighting her.

Her acute hearing sensed the waves of footsteps following her. Only one pair this time. Perhaps they've given up the sport of chasing her in groups? No, surely not, sports are too addictive. And chasing her seemed to have given the men something they could enjoy, something which held out the promise of worthwhile winnings. But no one had won yet, though many had bragged about it and even more had disappeared. It was this test of either/or which seemed to inspire a frenzied desire for winning in the men, as if going down in a raptured dream were worth the risk of death. But they would usually hunt her in packs minimizing the risk and increasing the possibility of reward in a gang slam. Occasionally someone would hunt her away from the pack. Once a contender, that man would usually disappear in a blood bath. Rarely did someone dare to hunt her alone like the man behind her now.

Lying down in a dale between two dunes she began to purr. Passing through the stages of turning into a panther started with her head as her skull folded over itself fusing upper and lower parts of her brain. Then her hands turned into claws as her spine pushed itself through her lower back transforming into a swaying tail. Curling up to her stomach, her legs turned into the panther's powerful hind legs, the left one decorated with a thin crescent moon created by a string of white hair where there used to be a scar. The history of the man following her was about to come to an end. She made a warning howl and smelled him freeze in fear two dunes away.

The clouds in front of the moon merged and total darkness descended on the beach.

She turned her head as the last ray of light hit the man. She saw that he was sitting down calmly, though the scent of fear still came from him. He was naked unlike the usual hunters who were most often dressed in skins or rags. He was handsomely built. Sturdy frame and an intelligent face, his eyes gleaming in the darkness. He was trying to penetrate the darkness with all his senses. She decided to take him from the back in a quick, quiet motion. He would feel nothing. She got up.

Certain that her trek in a large curve around the dunes was completely silent, she sat down six feet behind him. His white skin revealed his shape in the darkness. As a relief his back arched towards her. Holding her breath she got ready.

When she was in the air half way towards him he moved away in a fast lightning move and turned towards her as she landed on the spot still warm from his body. The smell of fear still emanated faintly from him. "I felt you coming," he said.

The moonlight broke through again as the two clouds passed each other moving to opposite sides, again framing the face in the sky.

She roared, ready to attack again. "Calm now, calm," he said. "Your fear is unwarranted. I'm not a hunter." She stopped, her instincts confused.

"The time has come for friendship," he said, "which is only possible with risk. I risk sitting here. It's your turn to risk. You are a sister of the moon and I am a brother. Togetherness is the next step. We are ready for this, you know. It's the stage we've come to."

Something was right about his words. She transformed again as he stood up and moved towards her. Standing up herself she said, "Your fear?" not understanding why it was still there. "Not because of you," he said, sighing with relief. Less than three feet apart the two naked humans began exploring each other with their eyes.

Their lips moved towards a kiss as the moon seemed to increase its intensity, spotlighting the lovers standing at the top of the highest dune.

Slowly moving away from her he said, "I'm sorry."

"What?" she gasped.

From the sand he drew a machete-sized knife, the blade sparkling in the moonlight. "It is time," he said, tears forming in his eyes.

"How could I not know?!" she screamed but before she could become a panther again the knife had cut through her neck, detaching her half human half panther head from the rest of her beautiful body. Her blood flowed silently into the sand where it fed a different world.

Standing in her footsteps on the beach he held her head towards the moon in his outstretched arm. "I've done as you wished," he shouted out over the ocean.

The clouds passed over the moon again, engulfing the beach in darkness and leaving the shark unseen to find his way back into the deep.

III

SOCCER MADE IN GERMANY

PER BRASK

THE YEAR THE LEAVES WERE SMALLER

GEORGE SZANTO

SOCCER MADE IN GERMANY

PER BRASK

It had sounded like a string breaking. A soft, muffled and peculiarly slow snap. He felt a wetness all over his body which he soon identified as sweat. He felt himself running on grass, he sensed that he was wearing shorts for as he moved through the air a breeze was created around his legs from just below his knees up to about the middle of his thighs. Then a second slow snap and he could see that he was running after a ball on a soccer field.

He was wearing a black and white striped jersey, black pants and black socks, as were some other players, and the ball that he was running after was just now being caught by a player in a blue jersey and white pants.

He felt himself stretching out at an angle, feet leading the way, gliding in front of the player with the ball. His opponent tripped over his calf, sending a numbing pain up through his spine. A split second later he felt the kick of a soccer boot in his lower back. His opponent was angry and was screaming at him but he couldn't make out the words. It was then that he heard an additional sound, a huge roar, also strongly muffled. He looked up and realized that he was lying in the middle of a large stadium watched by what looked like thousands of spectators, some cheering, some booing. How had he got there?

He couldn't get up. The kick in the back had incapacitated him. It hurt when he tried to move. The sound of a whistle reached him, then the thumping of heavy, running footsteps. His vision was blurring but he could still see the two men who put him on a stretcher and, when he turned his head as much to the side as the pain would allow him, that the black clothed referee was sending the player he had tackled off the field. Then he closed his eyes and all sounds disappeared.

When he opened his eyes again a few seconds later, everything was black and still, without sound. He tried to speak, then yell, but nothing came out. He tried to move, but there was nothing for him to move. His body seemed to have disappeared and he could not make one part touch another for nothing would obey his will, which was apparently all he had left. He felt helpless; what was happening? Was this caused by his injury? Had the tackle really been this violent? No, this had nothing to do with soccer. He felt that with an uncommon certainty, as if the questions had answered themselves before they even appeared in his mind.

Then he heard the sound of string breaking again. But this time the sound was even slower, so slow that the picture it conjured up in his mind was in such slow motion that he imagined seeing tiny particles of hemp splitting into dust and scattering in all directions. He started to feel a body again. It was different from the soccer player's. This one was heavier, a little flabbier, but more importantly, familiar. The pain and the sweat were gone. His vision started to return and he recognized his old grey pants and his yellowish cardigan over his light-blue shirt. He was back in his favourite and most comfortable chair in front of the television, where he now remembered he had been watching "Soccer Made in Germany" on PBS.

Then he heard the announcer interrupt the program to say, in a dismayed and confused voice, that the tackle and fight viewers had just witnessed had not taken place when the match was played last week, and that he had no way of explaining what kind of mix-up had occurred with the tape during transport. The player who'd been carried off on a stretcher was supposed to have scored three more goals, bringing his team into the leading position for the European Cup. But now. . ? The picture on the screen went snowy, then repaired itself, and Harold Petersen watched the game again from his "entry" through the injury to "his" team losing the match 3-1.

He sat stiff for a moment, wondering whether he had dreamt his experience, and just as he was deciding that of course he had, an unfamiliar but sweet voice called out "Dinner is ready, honey."

Harold got up from his chair quickly, but before he could say, "Who are you?" his mouth had formed the words, "Thank you." As he turned around he noticed with shock how his living room had changed. Though the furniture was more or less situated as he remembered, it was decidedly not his, that is, with the exception of his large comfortable La-Z-Boy and the television set. His furniture used to be basic, upholstered chairs and sofa from The Bay, and two teak tables he had bought second-hand after his divorce. What he was looking at was colourful pieces of cloth supported by steel or brass pipes shaped into what must be very pleasant positions, and the tables had glass tops. This living room was filled with flowers and plants he had never seen before, at least he could not recall right now that he had.

A beautiful woman appeared at the door to the kitchen. She had long black hair, large brown eyes, and high cheekbones. Her face was well made up and her red lips seemed uncontrollably desirous to Harold. Her red dress revealed the contours of a female shape he would not normally have dared dream could be accessible to him. Yet he knew that the woman in front of him was his dearly beloved, and he also knew that she loved him. He even knew her name, Carol. It tremored like an erotic whisper through his body.

Was he dreaming?

"What is the matter, darling?" said Carol. "You look pale." And before Harold could introduce himself and apologize for his confusion he had said, "I'm fine. I must've fallen asleep in front of the TV. Sorry, dear, I'm just a little groggy."

They went into the large kitchen designed in red ceramic tiles and exposed raw pine. Harold was not surprised because he had expected it to look different (after all the living room did), and because curiously he had begun to feel that although his environment had changed, both it and Carol fitted him better than what had existed before. In fact his memories of before were receding so quickly to the far back of his mind that when he kissed Carol before they sat down to eat, he sensed nothing new about the experience. On the contrary, he remembered having done so many, many times before. Indeed, she seemed a much more eager kisser than he, and this too felt natural to him.

As he sat across from her, eating a deliciously prepared leg of lamb, he noticed that this feeling of naturalness in his new life was increasing with enormous rapidity. By the time he cut into his second caramelled potato his only remaining uneasiness was whether he could afford this new life.

He must have said something out loud, because he suddenly heard Carol say, "You're so funny Rald, you always worry about money."

Rald? And yet, that too found a resonance. To Carol he was Rald, a nickname she had given him five years ago when they'd first started courting. She'd been a student of his, brilliant he thought, and they'd got married six months ago on the very day that she was awarded her Ph.D.

His environment and Carol no longer simply felt natural to him; they were also assuming a history. His new life, Harold felt, was no longer new, it had a past, it had interconnections with the rest of the world, past and present, which created its existence, his existence, in fact.

"Are you sure you're well?" asked Carol.

"Yes, yes, I'm fine."

"But we're not having much of a conversation, honey, I'd hoped that—"

"I am sorry sweetheart. I was just mentally going over notes for my lecture tomorrow. I didn't mean to be rude."

"It's all right. Did you read my paper?"

Harold had indeed read her paper and he was not surprised that he had, nor that he remembered it. For the rest of the evening they had a stimulating and fruitful discussion of Carol's paper, a study of the different social relationships to time before and after the French Revolution, juxtaposed with the synchronically similar but culturally different understandings of time in industrial North America and rural Latin America. The paper was entitled, "On the Epistemological Status of the Notion of Efficiency." Carol was to deliver it at a symposium two weeks later.

That night Harold experienced a kind of tenderness and discovery in lovemaking which, in another life he would have been unable even to fantasize, but which he knew had been his fortunate experience with wonderful regularity for the past four and a half years.

Harold Petersen loved his new life.

The next day he got up, put his notes together, and made breakfast before waking Carol. As he passed through the living room he noticed how odd his old La-Z-Boy looked in his new living room, and during breakfast he mentioned this feeling to Carol.

"Finally, you see it," she said.

"Finally?"

"We've argued about that chair for months, honey. I don't know why you want to keep it."

"I guess I think it's comfortable. It just doesn't look right in the room. We should get one that fits in."

"Are you sure?"

"Of course."

"And you don't mind spending the money?"

"Certainly not."

"Good. Saturday, when the furniture exhibit starts we'll go down and find something really special."

Harold went off to the university to give his lecture. It was attended by over five hundred students, all paying careful attention to his outline of the methodologies of historical research considered most valid. Only his voice could be heard in the lecture hall, and during his pauses one could have heard the proverbial needle drop. He was clearly an important and respected man.

The words, sentences, concepts, logical delineations and criticisms came freely out of his mouth. He knew what he was talking about and he also knew that he had obtained this knowledge through many years of hard work. Still he could not rid himself of a faint uneasiness at the seemingly automatic flow of the words. When he arrived home after his lecture Carol was out, at the library, a note said. After making a cup of coffee and an avocado sandwich, Harold went into the living room to read his mail and the morning newspaper. Barely had he sat down on the sofa, however, before he sensed the La-Z-Boy "beckoning" him. He looked at it and for a moment a body seemed to take shape in the chair. His shape. It never materialized clearly but he could make out the almost invisible outline. After it disappeared he sat looking at the chair. He could not get his eyes or his mind off it. The curious sensation that a memory was trying to force its way into his consciousness settled over him. It could not get through, despite hard fighting and his very best assistance. The memory, or thought, was kept out by an insuperable barrier but he knew that he could not, after all, separate himself from his favourite chair.

In bed that night he tried to explain how he'd changed his mind about the chair.

"Oh, no," she said. "I was really hoping we could finally make that room look decent."

"I'm sorry, honey."

"Well, I've always known you had strange quirks, but please reconsider this. I just can't stand that chair."

Harold promised to think it over again, but he knew that he and his chair were inseparable.

They didn't make love that night.

Carol didn't raise the issue of the chair again. Maybe she'd given in or maybe she was just very patient.

The rest of the week was filled with teaching, research and dinner parties. Three dinner parties were with very close friends and Harold knew them all extremely well, and discovered that he was very skilled at keeping university-related matters out of any conversation by being an interesting storyteller. At a fourth dinner party he was being awarded a large research grant but suddenly he could not remember what for, and when he was to give his speech of thanks he could not utter a word. Steel pipes, plastic pipes, box wrenches, socket wrenches and Allen wrenches mysteriously appeared in his mind. He began to cry and sat down again. Everyone present burst into thunderous applause and Carol hugged and kissed him. The great and respected scholar had shown himself to be human and was instantly better respected than ever. It was, however, for Harold, a devastating evening. As Carol kissed him he whispered almost silently in her ear, "Good-bye, my love." He didn't know why he said it nor did Carol seem to hear it for she did not respond.

The following day, on Sunday afternoon, Harold was again sitting in his chair in front of the television watching "Soccer Made in Germany" on PBS. He felt slightly queasy, but he was unable to get up from the chair and he did not want to disturb Carol, who was taking a nap. He tried to get up a couple of times but each time he felt more stuck than before. It was only when he gave up and sat back in his chair that he realized that the soccer match he was watching was exactly the same as the one he'd seen a week earlier. The panic left his body and he sat staring at the screen watching as the match moved towards the point where he had "entered" a week earlier. As he tried to raise his hand to turn off the TV he saw that his watch was running backwards with tremendous speed; seconds, minutes, hours and dates were turning back.

Then he heard the breaking string, and moments later, he was once again covered in sweat and dressed in a soccer uniform. His tackle was successful this time, and he passed the ball to his centre-forward, ran up the field, received the ball in a free position and scored a beautiful goal. At the exact moment the ball hit the net the string broke again.

Back in his chair he opened his eyes slowly as he heard the announcer praising the goal. His vision came back quickly this time and as he turned he found himself back in his old place. He wanted to call out Carol's name but no sound came.

The telephone rang. He got up to answer it, and as he was about to greet the caller with "Professor Petersen's residence," he heard himself say, "Petersen's Plumbing."

The caller wanted him to handle an emergency, and he promised to come over in five minutes.

Harold knew his new environment as well as the one which was now receding from his mind. However, as it disappeared, he was filled with anticipation as he looked forward to next week's match on "Soccer Made in Germany."

THE YEAR THE LEAVES WERE SMALLER

GEORGE SZANTO

Stand on a dock. Look into the water. Watch a perch hover, glide, hover, flip its tail, catch the light, disappear as you stare. You know it's still down there.

Think of the great fish, of the sea and in the rivers. They sink to the bottom of their waters in death or are tricked and caught for sport or are trapped unprepared in their turbulent homes by trawlers. Like the small perch, their disappearance, their obliteration, is not possible. Something is left, a gill, a scale, a spleen, a piece of memory, of fear; whatever cell.

So it was in earlier times.

He loved watching her on television, especially lying in her own living room, almost as much as he loved it when she and Uncle Bart took him along to the cabin; those were two of his favourite things. He had written this is his little notebook and some of the thoughts he put there he explained to his friend Reg. He said a couple of days before coming down, "It's their lifestyle that's so great. They go back and forth from their neat house to the cottage on the lake all the time. It's great, having two houses." Lifestyle was one of the words he'd picked up somewhere. He was asked where but couldn't remember, TV probably, and he liked to use it. He used words like that all the time. Some people said he was precocious. That irritated him. Being precocious was weird. He was smarter than Reg but he wasn't weird. Aunt Pat didn't think he was weird either.

A week before coming to visit he tried to get organized, prepare himself. Specifically, he asked for a raise in his allowance. Why? So he could buy his aunt and uncle a present. What? New red and white Dardevle spoons like the one he'd caught his twenty-three inch pickerel on last summer. His father took the money from his wallet—"When you're ten you get a hike, okay? Not till."—and made the usual noises about how could his sister and her husband possibly waste so much time fishing. Getting the money for the present straight out wasn't nearly as neat as being able to spend it from his allowance but at least he could buy the spoons. He'd gone down to Mission's Tackle on the bus by himself. He spent an easy hour judging and balancing the lures hanging from the wall—Flatfish and Riverunts, Wobblerites, Diveworms, the dozens of varieties and sizes of Dardevles. He knew exactly, weeks beforehand, what he'd buy, but facing the selection he stared, thought, remembered two, three moments from last summer. So he wasn't about to change his mind.

The red and whites were it, the great traditional Dardevle. One an inch and a half, one two inches. But some of the others held him, fascinated him; so many real possibilities, especially the Flatfish. An orange one with black spots, he could see it working through the water, slow slow retrieve, when it stopped it floated, the scoop-snout made it dive when you reeled the line in. And if you were really lucky you could see the pickerel or bass hit and start to swoop; then you set the hook, hard.

The shelves and hangers were full of gear. He bought the two he'd come for. His mind was instantly miles closer to the cabin. Through the last couple of weeks he'd already thought himself down to their house and to the lake at least a dozen times.

She was on live. He turned up the sound. He didn't know much of what she was saying but he listened hard. Last year, after, when he asked questions, she tried carefully to explain. It'd be important for him to be specific, she liked that. She was describing a volcano on the other side of the country, the first bunch of eruptions in years. A place called Mount St. Helens, two weeks ago, third time it erupted and the destruction went on and on, messing up logging camps and mining camps and all kinds of summer cottages people had. He was really glad there wasn't a volcano around his lake. Sickle was his lake, nearly his anyway because he loved it that much—his and his aunt and uncle's and the guy with the other place down the lake, those were the only people who had any right to Sickle. They'd head out soon as the show was done.

He liked seeing her face that way, surrounded by the blue background which made her eyes, they were blue too, seem to be looking only at him. Sometimes she did that when they were together; just for a couple of seconds though. On TV she seemed to be staring right into him, what he was thinking about and how the pictures in his brain moved from one kind of thing to another. That was okay, he liked to share that with her. He figured he knew better how to share with her than with his mother. Or father. Really even more than with his uncle. This didn't bother him, he loved his parents. But Auntie Pat was great.

She was only on for a couple of minutes. He wished she would've talked longer. Anyway now she'd be home soon. Her on TV, it made him feel important, his father's sister on TV and talking directly to him. He'd told Reg, "My aunt's on TV. On the news." He didn't tell Reg she wasn't on every night. He didn't write it in his notebook because it was hard to explain clearly and he didn't tell Reg either what she had told him, "It's not a real network TV station, it's just the hour we get to broadcast local news and a few times a week they give me a couple of minutes to editorialize." What's editorialize? Where she got her chance to say her opinion, explain how things worked. Didn't matter, when he saw her on the screen she'd be smiling, enjoying herself. And look the same after, when they talked. So it was an important program. Reg had asked, "How come I don't see her on our TV?" "Because you can't get that station without cable, stupid."

Ten minutes and she was there. "You packed?"

"Yep."

"I'll get my jeans on and we can go."

"Where's Uncle Bart?"

"Oh," she smiled a big grin, "he has to be away for the weekend, he was called down to New York, he's really really sorry."

"Oh." He felt himself pull in his cheeks and his shoulders go tight and his eyes got scratchy. "When will he get back?"

"Probably late Sunday. Come on, get your stuff."

It was all together, had been all afternoon, just another pair of jeans and a change of underwear and a change of socks, he wouldn't get dirty but he might get wet, all he needed. And the lures. What was he supposed to do with Uncle Bart's Dardevle?

They left at six-fifteen, got to Sickle by seven-thirty. They had talked long and seriously: should they fish till dark? They'd weighed the pros and cons. He liked her for that, she let him make the decision with her. Not what only he or she wanted but what was good and bad about all the choices. He wouldn't tell Reg about the decision-making or even write it down because it wasn't that clear. Anyway, afterwards you forget what the other choices had been. And Reg would only say either you do something or you don't.

But it was a lot more complicated. For example he liked the sitting around and talking in the evening. If they went out fishing it'd be a quick supper, cold things, cheese and peanut butter or something. Which was okay but one of the nice parts of being at the lake was the cooking. They had a wood stove and he'd help make up the fire, gather the wood first and then lay it, then get it to burn and cook soup on it or something. Everything always tasted better cooked on the wood stove. Except if they went right out fishing they'd have to forget all the other good parts.

They talked it through. And agreed not to fish that evening.

The cottage was silent and bright, somehow in the late light shinier than he remembered. The lake was motionless, a perfect mirror. They walked slowly out on the dock. They stood silent, stared at the water, its total peace. Somewhere a duck squawked. Fifty feet offshore a fish swirled. Definitely a big one. In his mind he could see it swim away barely a foot underwater, a grasshopper or maybe a minnow in its mouth. They could change their minds. "Auntie Pat, if we went out for half an hour—"

She was staring over the lake, above the trees on the other side, beyond the mountain far behind. Her teeth were biting her lower lip hard, her eyes were blinking, they looked bluer than he'd ever seen them, she didn't say anything.

"Should we maybe start the fire?"

She looked down at him slowly as if she hadn't heard till then. Which was okay because he didn't want her to think he felt like changing plans just because a stupid fish swirled while they were standing there and—She kneeled down, put a hand on his shoulder, looked at his face like she had on TV. Her eyes were glowing blue. They looked like his felt when he was about to cry. Suddenly she was hugging him hard, holding him like only twice before when she put him to bed when there were just the two of them in the house. She held tight like that, no movement, saying nothing. A fish jumped, it must have cleared the water completely it made that big a splash. She let go of him. "We'll get that fat feller tomorrow."

Her hand lay loose on his shoulder and they walked back from the dock together. He reached up and put his arm around her waist because he had to do something.

In earlier times an ancient pike is caught in the nets of a Lake Superior fishing boat. The pike thrashes left, under, sharply. But the net is too strong, its fibres too tightly meshed, the weave too flexible. It will not strain or tear. It has been, as men say, well-made; it holds. The fish is hoisted aboard with lines and gaffs. It lies for a moment panting on the deck, then is thrown in the ice-hold. Slowly its living processes depart. A man whets his knife. He will now, as he thinks it, clean the fish. When its lifeworks are cut away— its heart, its ballast, its bowels—then it is ready for market, for consumption.

There is still the other part: what is cut away. On the red deck or at the bottom of the lake, the carnage, useless to men, goes on: the bowel, the fin, the cheek. Regeneration begins. Not, of course, as living flesh; fish too follow material laws. No. The flesh of fear. With the result that new uncertainties, new questions have been loosed upon the world. Yes, as broad as that. The entire world. You cannot limit the flesh of fear to riverside towns or coastal villages.

How does it act, this flesh of fear?

Recall the perch, the dock, the pike. The fish disappears from sight. To feed on prey, as life begins again. The hour before, the hour after sunrise, these he prefers. Altered now, skulking behind the shadows of stones, hovering in the half-light, at grey edges where the mind has forgotten it is naked, there he is, ready to flash out from the beds and grooves of streams of thought or fancy, from our sunken uncertainties. Up he leaps. Where light begins to play, hopeful, with the old dark branches, shadows, overhanging bushes. There.

At the finish of day, light fading, there too. They are stealthy beasts. Their appetites are reborn in the hour of twilight as tree limbs leaning out from the shoreline darken this deep world, branch after branch creeping low into the water, hiding their search, their movement. Nights with clouded moons are best.

We who move in air are not prepared for fishlike acts. In our warm beds we nudge our way toward sleep, numb to the departed fish. But suddenly we know. They are here, beneath our surface, in the deep. Will we look? Do we want to? We stir, fitfully. Is silence of any use now? We have to move, so long as we breathe we have to move. On the surface all is quiet, motionless, dark. Sleep will come, surely.

It must.

The boy woke when the grey light came into his window. The blanket was warmer than he remembered, it felt pretty good. He looked. She'd spread a quilt on top of him too. She was great. He stuck his foot out. Cold in the room, cold as winter. Almost. He thought about changing his mind; this was no day to go searching. Or maybe wait till later. No, later was for fishing. Besides, she deserved it. Even more now, putting on the quilt. It'd have to be a leap, a jump into the clothes, pull on socks and sweatshirt. Why were the clothes so far away? Last night hadn't he put them next to the bed so he could get dressed under the covers? He'd get up, bring them back under, warm them up, and then—Wasn't worth it. He remembered from last year once you were up it was okay. He'd have sworn he left his clothes by the bed.

He got up and dressed and was quiet and sneaked past her room and opened the door really silent. He hadn't thought about being cold and realized he was cozy warm out on the cool porch. The dew in pearls on the railing soaked into floor planks where they needed a coat of stain.

Up from the cabin, on the hill where it gets sun all day, last year there were five bushes full of wild pink roses. He'd picked a present for Auntie Pat and Uncle Bart, a huge bouquet, maybe thirty stems, and it didn't even look like he'd taken a single one, so many were left on the bushes. He'd find them again even without the sun up, anyway the bushes would be about the first place the sun hit. The grass was wet and matted and his sneakers were soaked, his socks too, but it didn't matter because his feet were warm and the wet sneakers acted like insulation.

He got to the middle of the hill. His jeans were wringing wet which wasn't so nice, they flopped heavy against his shins and where the air got at his legs they felt cold and clammy. The roses were here somewhere, probably harder to see before sunrise, the buds'd be all folded up till the sun opened them. He found a patch of bushes, he thought this was the right place; a few branches, half a dozen maybe, ended in flowers; scrawny, weird-looking. Maybe they'd come and gone? His wet legs gave him a shiver of a chill. Maybe he'd gone to the wrong place. Last year Uncle Bart'd shown him where the roses were and this year Uncle Bart wasn't here. No, that made no sense either. The place didn't feel right. Like shadows were hiding the roses away.

Trees live in their roots, in the dark. Above they shade us with their leaves and branches, show us where to tap through their bark for syrup, we pick their fruits, admire their colour; breathe their oxygen. Beneath all this, in its hidden roots, a tree finds its largest world, it joins with other trees, with plants, with soil, with rocks, with underground streams. The roots go deep if the tree is old, has lived through seasons of rainlessness and seasons of heat. The tree knows the worms well, they open the soil, letting water in from above and up from below. A small root will spend its life pushing against hard soil but will sink easily down in the burrows of worms. Below ground, too, trees come to know the gopher, the fox, the rabbit; below ground animal and plant together feel the daily surges coming from the surface. In recent years the world above has grown strange; the wolverine and the possum tell of forage disappearing, of strange new scents in the air, scents not familiar from the tales of ancestors or the browsing of elders in their early days.

Below, down deep, where earth meets water, the fish speak to the roots of the great trees. Their stories have changed in many ways from those stories formed beyond memory; because the old stories, once true, now seem fanciful and foolish even to the teller; changed, because the waters have changed. The fish speak to the roots, roots glide over scales and fins in the waters, but even here sound and touch have grown feeble. The fish which have always spread their knowledge cleanly, glasslike, now find they must explain themselves. Never before in the world's history has a fish needed more than a flash of its gill plate, the fish have always been understood; as has every root. Once it was sufficient to live and simply die, to become again the carbon and the water and the protein which had made them; or even to be held and eaten by humans, then in the flesh of memory to linger, regenerating, inside this man, that child, all life long. This was how it had been.

But ease has fled from the waters where root and fish commune. Long ago protein and carbon and water re-formed, new fish were created, new of the old and with new transformations; and a boy would learn, despite his teachers and his parents, that he did not understand the way the world was made, not all of it, not the places of fear. But now? Now the great fish have lost their potency, and their regenerative powers. Why? How? And what will they do? Where can they find again the deep current which from the first days has let them live, die, recombine in later eons with other particles to become new life, new force? It could not happen near the surface. Would they need to go deeper, into the roots, below?

She was awake and frying up blackberry pancakes. They smelled terrific. He was chilled, shivering. Butter and maple syrup already on the table— He had nothing to give her. Last year was better. "Hi!" Though this year they could talk together, the two of them alone.

"Boy, are you soaked! Out wading after fish?"

"I went for a walk."

"Well go on, get changed. Want hot chocolate?"

"Yeah!"

They were on the lake half an hour after sunrise. They had their ritual: if they trolled he took the motor even while working his rod. If they were rowing, casting, she took the oars, positioning them by a good spot, let the boat drift while they worked the water. They rarely spoke on the boat, the jokes and the kidding were for land. Out here you paid attention. She'd point to a hawk on a branch or raccoons cracking open fresh-water mussels against rocks or tree roots where somebody, probably the guy from across the lake, had snagged a rig and torn it off. Always she gave him the good place to cast even if it looked easy from her angle. Or he'd point to a hollow or a weed-bed where a foot and a half pickerel had to be waiting lazily for a crayfish, or for a baby duckling to swim innocently by overhead— Cast it there, Auntie Pat, get that feller. If they did and it was big enough he'd net it for her, or she for him.

At least he figured that was the agreement. Last year he didn't have to do the netting since Uncle Bart had been with them.

She was fishing a June-bug, a silver and red spinner trailing a black and white bucktail. She'd loaned him her favourite Flatfish, the orange with black dots. They'd drifted into a small bay that usually produced something. He looked up suddenly. "Hey, that tree didn't used to be there."

It lay over to the right, once the biggest tree on the bay, an old beech fallen into the water, dividing the little inlet one-third, two-thirds. It once stood a couple of feet back from the water edge; now on its side, the network of its roots reached six feet into the air. From the boat's angle they could see the hole the roots had left, a grey hollow where rock sloped up from the water.

She said, "Maybe it'll help," and cast between two branches, sodden, bare of life. She retrieved in jerks, letting her June-bug imitate a wounded minnow. Nothing. She cast again, a little farther in, slowed the retrieve, worked it up almost to the surface, let it drop. Nothing. Tried the point where the newly barkless tree met the shoreline, a neat cast into the pocket three feet in diameter, worked it slowly, skipped it over some weeds.

He watched the retrieve, hoping for her. There ought to be a big one lurking by those underwater branches. She cast so beautifully. He had worked on precision back home, casting a rubber plug out to a garbage can. He was getting better but he'd bet she could flick a cigarette from somebody's mouth with a quarter-ounce practice weight. He'd seen that once on TV. She was that good.

Except now her perfect casts didn't help and the downed tree hadn't improved the bay. Maybe even spooked the fish.

"It'll get better when the water warms up. Want a sandwich?"

Barely two hours since breakfast but casting was hard work and the fresh air had gotten to him, no question. He knew he wasn't hungry but he nodded, grinning; she wanted eating company and also she liked it when he gobbled down her sandwiches. She was quiet this morning like always, but quiet in a different way.

After the bay there was a rocky stretch where they usually trolled. They'd caught a couple of good walleye there last year. Now they agreed on the same tactic. He took the motor, a responsibility that gave him a lot of pleasure. He steered carefully to keep them from stalling and still going slow enough for any fat walleye to see her Scutterbug and his Wob-L-Rite. He finally had a hit, a good one, set the hook— Nothing there. Then she had a strike and felt it on, wound it in like it was a piece of weed. In fact she said, "Lily pad." But it was a fish, an eleven-inch perch, no need for a net. She held it half out of the water, wet her hands, squeezed the knife-sharp gills shut and released the hook. "Skinniest perch I ever saw."

They trolled some more. Nothing. A bad-luck fishing day; morning, at least. It didn't matter. He loved being out on the water, loved being her fishing partner.

It would've been better if she'd been happier; or at least looked happier. She didn't usually get like that when they didn't catch. Last year just being out on the water with her and Uncle Bart had been enough. He figured the time was probably right so he took the wrapped package, the bigger one, from his tackle box and handed it to her. "I got you this."

She opened it, saw the two-inch Dardevle, best lure going, took it out of its plastic covered case. Squeezed it in her hand. Closed her eyes as if she wanted to get a clear feel of it, its weight, this present from her nephew who understood how much she loved this lake, its freedom. She took his hand and held it to her cheek. She opened her eyes and smiled. The smile looked wrong, off. Still it was a smile, he'd managed to do that much.

Below the roots, below the soil, below the waters, below the fish, below the mud and the stones, there is the world's own warmth. It is a sweet warmth but we know it poorly, as from mines smelling of sour sweat blended with coal dust, or from the fetid air of spas. It is an energizing warmth, born of steam deep beneath the crust layers, the barest fraction of which our science claims to understand. Coming from a place before men, before trees, before fish, before water, but a place known to the fish now because they have learned of it from the deepest mud. To the water they have spoken of the trees, how the trees have left, are leaving. The water in its fog of steam has hissed of these departures to the heat below mud and stone. The heat has asked, What is this thing which makes the trees depart? The trees in their roots have told of particles in the air which their leaves do not know. Cannot breathe. Cannot absorb. Why? What is all this? There is no answer.

The heat in the earth then asks, And what will happen to the leaves? There is no answer. The fires in the depths know very little, but they do know this: so long as what is taken away is also given back, so long as the layer that shields the fires remains in balance, flames will appear on the surface only from the cones of volcanoes, never from those fissures carved by themselves.

When is the moment of combustion? There is no answer.

But if the underlayer, the waters, the roots, the fish, the mud, if all this is awry, if the world's balance is undone, then the fires of the deep will feast on the impurities, the core will become a ravenous beast, the fires will climb to the surface through worm holes and rabbit holes, along roots and up mine shafts, along thermal springs and from the depths of volcanoes, will blast and rage through faults and fissures, will thrust aside miles of coastal shield as if this were the petals of a drying flower.

When? For how long?

There is no answer.

In the late afternoon, about five, they fished a thick patch of lily pads at the far end of the lake, the shallow end where a stream came in. Water lilies, white here, yellow beyond, were beginning to poke their bowls out of the water.

"Aren't they lovely."

He didn't think she wanted an answer. Lots more lily pads than last year. Aunt Pat said because of the logging back in spring lots of garbage must've got dumped and it washed into the lake when the snow melted, like fertilizer it made the water lilies grow. The stream was a lot wider than last year when they'd had a picnic there but it had less water. Anyway it looked wider, maybe you could see better without the trees.

He cast into the black surface next to some broad green pads. He was using the same Flatfish, working it along the edge of the pads, slow retrieve, very slow, sink a little, then floating again, a jerk and it went under. He could see it clearly the surface was so windless. He turned to her and started to say, "Do you—"

She said, "Look."

He turned his head, the barest of motions. Back of the Flatfish floated a small log, maybe two feet long. Except it had a tail. The tail flicked lightly, sometimes under the water sometimes just dimpling the surface. The pickerel drifted as the Flatfish drifted. The boy waited, readied himself. He whispered, "Now." He flicked his rod-tip lightly, the Flatfish dived to six inches and forward maybe eighteen. It was still moving when the pickerel, faster than the tug on the line, grabbed it sideways. The boy set the hooks, the hooks bit into bone.

The fish fled along the side of the jungle of pads, searching for its entrance. The reel drag sang. The pickerel changed tactics, dove, arced up, leapt high, flashed its tail and rattled its head, shone mottled green and black, gills blood-red in the slanted sunlight, dropped back, sped through mudgrass but in a curve now. The boy saw the line head for a near clump of lilies, he held on hard, straining the line to its full test strength, turned the fish, reeled now. Now the fish swam slowly, with jerks and yanks, widely to the boat.

She got the net ready. "He'll run again."

"I know."

Seven feet from the boat, seeing it, the fish turned right. The end of its energy took it fifteen feet as the click-drag whined away; then the fish was spent. A few puffs and pulls, a pass with the net missing, a final dive under the boat as the boy deftly brought his rod round the bow so she could take him on the other side. She scooped, lifted, up, over the gunwale, in. He flopped, thrashed about in the net, knocked the hooks loose.

"Great," she said.

"Look at him," he said, "his belly."

It was a beautiful fish. The pointed head scowled mightily at the world, its flesh was firm beneath the two-foot-plus spangle of green-black skin. Its belly was classically yellow-white. Except instead of the usual straight yellow-white line the rear section down by the anal fin was distended. Huge. Bloated. Round as if it'd swallowed a tennis ball. Whole. Couldn't digest it. The boy thought, the fish is trying to poop out a tennis ball and it's got stuck.

"I don't think we better eat this one," she said.

They didn't feel much like more fishing. She said she'd brought steak along. They could have a fire outside if he'd like. He didn't, much.

He took himself for a walk. Up on the little hill he stared down at the cabin, beyond to the lake. A fish splashed. He saw the spreading dying circles. It all looked like last year. Maybe a little different. The woods weren't as thick as before, more light was coming through. He hated the big pickerel. Auntie Pat had said it wasn't the pickerel's fault, probably something he'd eaten. Not a tennis ball though. They'd both tried to laugh. He just wished the pickerel had been okay. Wished he could make it okay. Couldn't think of how. Auntie Pat had been so sad he'd asked her, "What's the matter, have I done something wrong?" When she stayed silent a long time he said, without planning to, "Or Uncle Bart?" she'd given him one of those looks with her blue blue eyes. Behind her face the sky was just as blue. "After a while it's just out of control," she'd said. He'd guessed he understood then. Now he figured, sitting up on the hill, he'd give her the second Dardevle too.

The fish hover. Their tails glide in the current. For balance? The thin water passes, flows away, silent. The memories, the roots, the fires wait.

IV

THE MAN WHO LOST NOUNS

GEORGE SZANTO

DEVILS

PER BRASK

THE MAN WHO LOST NOUNS

GEORGE SZANTO

At the party he can stay only a few minutes because they are due for late dinner at his parents' home. He sips watered scotch and cannot for the very life of him remember the name of the woman approaching. She has the sharpest wit he has ever encountered. Her political punditry on television earns her celebrity status, even notoriety. Till two years ago they'd been together for seven intimate months; their love made them a unit, he used to say. Her name is gone now. They parted amicably enough so there is no repression here; in a major career move she went out to the coast. Later, when he told Sandra about her, her name was still automatically there. Sandra had said, "I know about her, I've watched her show." In two seconds he will have to introduce them.

"Sam! Sammy!" The woman is all warm smile, genuine as ever it seems, and much shining thick black hair. In the embrace she gives him, he her, her scent brings back moments of their times together, walking side by side, sitting across restaurant tables, late evening rendezvous. But no name.

"This is wonderful—!" Work, mind. "How long's it been, two years?" Find, brain! "This is my friend Sandra—"

From Sandra: "Hello," reaching out her hand.

The other woman takes it—

An instant of silence—so brief only he can have felt it?—till: "I'm Deirdre Deerborn," and for the moment the problem is overcome.

"Yes, I've seen you lots of times and I . . ." begins Sandra's fine piece of grace and sends their silence into lost memory.

This happens to everybody, doesn't it? Everyone tells him so. Certain people remember names well, others badly. What shame in showing some human failing once in a while?

He can remember exactly when his, as he thinks it now, case began. Just over a year ago at the meeting after Thanksgiving of the International Immunology Association in Tehrān, in some grand salon, he had to introduce to each other associates from three parts of his life, one who'd been his professor at Harvard, another now his colleague at the General, the third he'd just been on a panel with for pity's sake! and he couldn't remember a single name. He laughed it off, jet lag. Which then he believed. They teased him for the next three days. Though not a man who welcomes teasing he allowed this because it was easier than straight-out admitting he'd lost their most valued possessions, their names. Nor could he place the kind of naked feeling that came with the forgetting.

It happened again, after Tehrān; first occasionally, more recently more often. A month ago he could not find the name of Sandra's son, her stepson, the boy's leg had just been amputated at the knee, leukemia, and he wasn't able to remember the kid's name. Of course he has it ever since, deeply etched in; Tyke. Short for Talbot Carter Robinson III. Sandra had cried a long time. Sam had rarely felt more awful. True, that piece of forgetting had its productive side, made him spend more time with Tyke. Time with Tyke makes his daughter Midge's absence more bearable too.

In the summer his case turned to nouns other than names, to just plain substantives. Since late November, five weeks now, he has lived with Sandra though they have been together for about sixteen months. When he admits he sometimes forgets names—he is able to, finally—he can, newly, laugh at how clever he is to live with a woman whose initials are copies of his, S.B.; or he might even forget what he is called. With Sandra if there is time for real talk he doesn't hide the new phase, this intrusion of the more general blank spaces. As half an hour ago on the drive to the party: "The trouble with Dimmesdale using that damn postoperative drug, none of us know its—its—" (toxicity) "how dangerous it might be, in the side effects." He was silent, then controlled his anger with a quiet, "Damn."

Or with the toast he had to propose last week at his annual pre-Christmas party, a small thing just for the core people: "To health. To the health of all of us at the General, to the health of our families, to the health of those like ourselves downwind from Three Mile Island, to the health of all who need not be unhealthy. And to the health of America's economy, so that our—our, uh—our" (benefactors) "so those who feel they should contribute to the immunology wing will recognize the spiritual as well as fiscal benefits of giving so they may also receive. Especially at the end of the tax year." Restrained laughter and applause. He'd almost managed to get the rhythm back. But not quite. Those tiresome, uh, contributors always threw him off. One way or another.

In the small acts of daily life as well. Telling a joke to his mother, say. Or explaining to the mechanic at the garage he thinks he has a crack in the, uh (manifold) you know, the pipe that all the others come into. Damned car, couldn't be trusted.

Sandra tells Deirdre they are expected right now at Sammy's parents. Deirdre says to Sandra, teasing Sam, "Sammy's a great guy, good to have around. When he's around, that is." The three laugh.

For a year-plus he has played with his forgetting only as a joke; has had to, how else to cope with it. This recent Thanksgiving—and he always thanks whatever gods might be lurking that the Iran conference had been last year, he pities those poor hostage bastards out there more than he can explain—he had tests through a doctor friend in New York. Far enough away from the General so nobody knew. A tiny stroke? A c.v. accident? The most realistic fear had been early Alzheimer's. But there is nothing, not a hint of a symptom. Except of course the forgetting. The friend suggested a shrink. They talked about it for a while. No, a slight case of dysphasia here, a shrink wouldn't be much help. The forgetting has forced onto Sam the beginnings of his sense of humour. A plus.

Sandra drives. "You look wiped out."

"Just tired."

Tentatively: "Did you drink much?"

"In thirty minutes? I held onto a glass of scotch. Maybe three sips. All the ice melted."

Drinking had been one of their few areas of disagreement. When they met he was relying on it a lot more than anyone should. True, they'd found each other just after the death of his sister Lucy, she one of the two hundred seventy-five killed in the crash of the DC-10 at O'Hare when one of its engines fell off; she and Sam had been very close as kids. In recent months the taste of alcohol is much less satisfactory. Wine sometimes; but it has to be fine; preservatives induce thudding headaches. He wonders if serious drinking has become one of the things he can no longer do. Booze had seemed the only way to forget exploding gases, burning metal, people—

Sandra touches his arm. "You'll be dazzling for Rosie?" Rosie is Sandra's bonus. Loving Sammy is grand. Falling for Rosie, and Rosie for her, ties Sandra into the family nice and solid. "As much fuss as you can." Rosie, whose real name is Emma but who relabelled herself at eighteen after the flowers she delights in because she hated Emma and has lived as Rosie for sixty years, Rosie loves to be dazzled; one of her favourite words; and moments. And needs these moments now more than ever. Last year Sam's colleague Dwight who people said had the finest hands at the General and about the best in the northeast told Rosie he was pretty sure he'd got the whole of it; but you can never be certain; five years would tell all. Rosie'd laughed. In five years the world might come to an end. Tonight they are bringing her a dozen long-stemmed roses.

"I'll dazzle. I promise." And for Pop he'll whittle up edges of irony just sharp enough so in any talking of Pop's old friends or enemies Sam's conversation will cut right to the little place where the old man's anger and jolly vindictiveness and sense of humour meet. Sam will make Pop more proud of him, more gut-pleased with him than any number of honorary degrees or headships of medicine ever can.

Sandra smiles, touches his hand, the pads of her fingers light on his skin. Has she just felt Sammy shift away from her?

He will dazzle. As long as the words come when needed. He will entertain.

"You and Deirdre must have been a dazzling pair too." No rancour here, Sandra knows a good deal about Sammy and Deirdre. He has told her, been she thinks as honest as he can, and she believes it all. They would have been remarkable with each other; Deirdre, beautiful—even more in person, remarkable skin, eyes, cheekbones—and brilliant; Sam, handsome yes though more correctly distinguished, in his mid-forties, eleven years head of the General and when he started the youngest ever, tasteful innovator, synthesizing researcher, tireless fundraiser; available divorced genius.

"Oh yes. Yes we were. Everybody who saw us said so. We weren't seen often." There had not been a lot of social time with Deirdre.

Sandra knows she and Sam make a less dazzling duo, that she is not a dazzling person; nor wants to be. She doesn't denigrate herself, she is very pretty at thirty-six. Sammy says she is lovely and she believes she is for him. She is also more for him; she is there, and waiting. He is now her life, he and Tyke. "She's really a remarkable human being." She had liked Deirdre; she knows this.

That, remarkably, seems to Sam well put; close to exact. Deirdre is, in a physical and intellectual sense, an acme. Others are compared to the Deirdres and judged thereby, the—the— (prototype) hell the, uh, model against whom other woman are measured; and measure themselves. Sam recognizes this now. Also since the time of Deirdre he's realized his notion of himself and her as a unit was really false. Together they were, at bottom, both alone. True, each shining brightly toward the other; even, to push it that far, reflecting each other's brightness. First he had felt elated with her, for a while proud. When she announced Los Angeles, relief. Somewhere he'd lost the pleasure she once gave him, that illusion.

"Surprise!"

Truly it is. He has not seen Midge since the end of the summer, the week before Labour Day. Midge's mother, Sam's one-time wife Helena, had given Midge that time with her father after camp ended. Did Midge fly down from Boston all by herself?

"Yep. And Grampop picked me up. All by himself."

All his life Pop has hated airports: flight is unnatural, against gravity. Teasing him about this quirk was once a family sport. Then in May the crash with Lucy on board. . . . But Midge, high on travelling alone, hasn't made the connection here. Pop breaks the tiny silence. "Only for you, Midgie." Yes he drove all the way into Philadelphia and out the other side to get to the plane. Pop is, always had been, a sucker for kids. "Because they keep fooling you," he would say. "Take Midgie. You think you've got a sense of what she's all about, you figure you can see where she's going, and whoof she's gone—but not where you figured." Only trouble is, he'll tell you, other people's kids you can't follow up on. Now relations, they'll go on coming back, surprising you. Till they're in their mid-teens; then they settle down, get boring. Most of them. Midgie he figures may keep shifting on him.

Midge had changed since Labour Day. Partly the new short haircut— "Like it?" She bounces her head in front of Sam barely a minute after he's arrived. "I got it for you." He'd have sworn right then she was flirting with him, the way Helena used to years ago. But Midge is hardly a year into double-digit age, what does she know about flirting? "So you just better like it." Which now is unadorned pout, a kid's; which puts Midge back in some recallable perspective. Not entirely, though. She is growing up and he hasn't been around to watch the little pieces of the process.

It is a good place, this big old-fashioned living room, lots of corners and a blazing crackling fire so three or four groups can talk quietly and be pretty much private. Good too because he's grown up in it and the feel is right, fitting around him a lot like the old green dressing gown he keeps upstairs. The only obvious addition is a stereo he gave Pop and Rosie for their fiftieth. With it on, like now, those corners are even more secluded. A good kind of intimacy, like for Sandra and Rosie over by the bay window speaking probably in a normal tone and he can hear only an occasional buzz and giggle. A fine thing, Sandra and Rosie. Pop has bought roses too, sweethearts, and their perfume mixes teasingly with the wood smoke.

Midge's long dress must be part of the change in her presence. Together with that no-nonsense responsibility helping Pop get drinks. "How many lumps of ice, Daddy?"

"Three."

"Won't that make it watery?" She wrinkles her brow, not easy to do with her smooth white skin.

She did seem—sound—more mature. "That's the way I take it these days."

"Better for you." She is off, accountable to her duties.

The house that makes the fewest demands. The people he loves best. The room that withstands the ravages of time. About the only thing Rosie has changed in the last ten years, praise the little devils who put the thought in her head, is she'd taken off those damn, uh, those—those, damn it! (antimacassars) little hair-oil protection doily things from the tops of the armchairs. What the hell are they called. Who needs them anyway, hair-oil for God's sake. For that moment it depresses Sam beyond explainable reason, not finding the word; this particular word, this evening. He shrugs away the moment.

"So, you decided?"

"What?" Sam knows what. He talked with Pop for over an hour last week. Pop forced him, for this first time, to make the pro and contra arguments out loud: take another six-year headship? or hand it on? "Haven't had time to think, really."

"Here's your scotch, Daddy."

"Thanks, Midge. You finished serving? Come talk to me."

"Just Rosie and Sandra. Be right back."

Midge and the directorship are the same age. She was born days after he first sat at the big desk. He and Helena had been married two years. When he took on the job it proved itself a mistress, a passion. A six-year affair, Helena had joked. But at the beginning of its final year he had said yes, he would take on another term.

Helena had said, "It's the affair or me, Sammy."

Sam had said, "I'm just beginning to make the dinosaurs see I'm right."

Helena had taken Midge. The divorce went through easily. He wanted to have Midge around but couldn't contest the reality, that he was home so little. At first living alone was no different.

Pop says, "You don't want to talk with Sandra about it?"

"There hasn't been a minute. I told you I'd worry it through soon, right?"

"Well, I've thought about it."

"Must be nice, having that kind of time."

"You make it or you lose it, Sammy."

"I know." He wishes he knew how. Come on Sammy, dazzle. How can you dazzle on the surface when underneath it's all—all—

Damn!

"Careful or you'll get to be older'n me."

"Careful of you'll get to be too wise for your own good."

"Just go back to your research. It's what you're best at, you know."

Best Sam doesn't know. But pretty good, yes. For the last eleven years there has not been a lot of time. He keeps up on the literature. And five respectable papers of his own, including Tehrān. He could get back quickly. This new immunity deficiency thing was fascinating, that you could so to speak catch it. It gets to the core of why he opted for immunology in the first place: prevention of disease, what medicine should be mostly about. And this new syndrome, that it was surfacing with increased frequency, well now that was intriguing. . . . "Maybe I will, Pop. Except I really do worry about that brontosaurus Dimmesdale maybe taking over." The right kind of threat: how to make Pop understand. Because Dimmesdale had once treated Pop, seventeen years back. Dimmesdale, all cut and slash, wanted to open Pop up, take a look. Because he'd heard Pop's heart murmur he said, glug-glug loud; maybe do a by-pass. Pop said it felt like indigestion, big gollops of gas. The EKG had shown an irregularity, sure, but that'd been there for years, since he was twenty-five. Sam recommended McLean who gave Pop his "little pink pills" and Pop's been fine ever since.

"Dimmesdale. Yeah. But surely to God there're other possibilities. No? Stop worrying about mistakes somebody else might make."

Except Sam has to, that's how his whole mind is constructed he tells himself over and over. Setting up an administrative structure that minimizes mistakes is a kind of immunology too. If only you could vaccinate against stupidity. "Look, Sandra's taking me off for three whole days. Time enough then for thinking. And talking. Okay?"

Pop is about to growl something else but Midge comes to sit on Sam's lap so this part of the argument is over. Sam wonders for a moment, for the evening? but Midge is talking about school which is easier to deal with.

"Well then you ask him." Rosie smiles.

Sandra shrugs. "I suppose I could." She pretends to mull this, as if for the first time. "Except maybe I'm a little old-fashioned. It should be the man that asks."

"But you've talked about it." She knows they have. What Rosie can't figure is, how do they go about first of all discussing marriage and second of all living together without third of all one asking the other, Do you want to? or even, Will you marry me? With normal people it simply has to be part of that kind of conversation. Sandra not answering, not saying the obvious, suddenly makes Rosie uncomfortable. "You've told me you have, Sandra. What's up."

"Oh. Nothing." She sighs. This is what Rosie is so good at, reading her. Nobody does that as well as Rosie, not even Sammy.

"Come on. Before dinner. Get it out. Dinner has to be fun."

"Rosie, I just don't know sometimes. I love Sammy so much, he's everything for me. Well, and Tyke—"

"What don't you know?"

"He's—I can't put my finger on it, really. Now and then I think I've got him pegged, what he wants, how he's feeling. And I adjust. I really do. I adjust to that. And before I know it, he's not there, he's gone somewhere."

"Gone? Left?"

"No, not left the room, I mean he's gone a lot of the time but I can deal with that, I don't have a Helena syndrome, it's not like that. No. . ."

"Then?"

"He sort of keeps shifting around on me. Like I start talking to one man and suddenly somebody else is there. Or at least a different part of him." She doesn't have a better way of saying this. "Know what I mean?"

It saddens Rosie. Not the shifting, Sammy's done that since he was a little boy. Less as a grown-up, a man. . . No, the sad part is this upsets Sandra so.

Pop looms. "Another drink?"

"I'm fine, Pop."

"Dinner's just about ready."

"Okay." Pop leaves.

The moment for Rosie to mention the sadness is gone now. The sadness itself stays, it washes through her. For Rosie the disappearance, of late, of normal bits of clarity is strange. Last week, last month, could she have tracked down Sandra's moment, recaptured it? Is there still something inside her, weakening her? Is that what keeps her from seeing and thinking clearly? What kinds of new categories is she going to have to create? At her age, for pity's sake. It is as if there was—how to imagine it?—something like a well that the sadness comes out of. She's been to this well a lot recently, it never goes dry. She wonders if the sadness itself, this piece of it for Sandra, may be keeping her now from speaking to Sandra.

Sandra does not know if Rosie sees what this shifting means.

Why does Rosie say nothing, why no explanation, at least hypothesis, for Sammy's moods? Sandra guesses he's caught: "Between wanting to stay on as director and really getting into this new research area. I think he's sort of jumping back and forth. In his mind."

How much more complicated. "Have you talked about that? The shifting?"

"He doesn't know what I'm talking about."

Hard for Rosie not to smile. No, Sammy doesn't ever see himself make the shifts. His weakness. But it leaves him room for greater insight elsewhere.

Pop brings Sam his refill. Midge says, "Grampop, you put in too much booze."

"Young lady you are too young to call my single malt whiskey *booze*."

She giggles. Sammy hugs her. Pop leaves them alone. For half a minute they are silent: he because he feels at peace, he has his little girl again, not forever but right now he settles for right now; she because her father has become older since the summer, he looks the same but she has suddenly forgotten how to talk to him, no that's all wrong too except if she says anything she'll start crying, she doesn't know why but her eyes get all watery, she has to force those tears back down—

Dinner is perfect, turkey, mashed squash, chestnut stuffing, champagne going on forever. Everyone is jolly. Much laughter, even some singing. Two glasses for Midge and over the chocolate cake she says she wants to lie down, just a bit, she won't fall asleep but if she does they have to wake her for midnight, promise? Promised.

Midge is gone. All four see clearly that the girl was their reason for the surface brightness, the jokes, songs, memories, teasing. It is the first New Year's without Lucy. Sandra never knew Lucy but has been infected by their mood. And drains up some of her own. How much is she part of, how separate from, this group? People, right here, she has come to love. Who are far away right now. And will return when? Under her skins she cringes: we all surge forward into the next decade and we don't feel a thing.

Sam describes this strange new disease, an acquired immune deficiency syndrome. They laugh with minimal humour at the acronym. "But because you lose your immunity to diseases of various sorts, you can't really call this syndrome itself a disease."

"People die of it, don't they?" Rosie doesn't like to speak these days of death but conversations often head that way.

"Look. People, animals, even plants have their own immune systems. Okay? They create them for themselves, I don't mean each person, I mean over a long period of time, generations, eons."

Pop disapproves when Sammy pontificates. "So how come there aren't any more dinosaurs around."

"Dimmesdale."

Pop and Rosie laugh.

"Okay, now when you get sick in some way, often it's as much the inability of the structure to withstand the destructive forces it's taken in as it is the external imposition of a disease. Okay?"

No one is speaking, not even nodding.

Sam feels now like he is on a tangent moving away from the centre with such incredible speed—

Rosie says, "Then my little malignancy came because my immune system couldn't stop it from growing happily there on my colon." Her voice is neutral.

"No. I mean, partly. What I mean is, there're all kinds of causes in the environment for cancer, the filth you breathe in and the junk in the food, and after a while the body can't cope with all of it any more. In that sense, yeah, the immune system one day can't handle the bulk. Well this AIDS thing looks like a bigger version of that breakdown."

Sandra whispers, "Sammy—"

He doesn't hear. "Everybody carries cancer viruses, various kinds, around with them all their life long. Only when one of the cancer immune systems breaks down, that's when the viruses attack and the carcinoma develops."

Sandra speaks loudly now: "Can we please talk about something else?"

Rosie gets up, starts to clear. "I think that's a good idea."

Sammy says, "I'm sorry, everybody. Really sorry."

Rosie loads the dishwasher. Sammy, businesslike, helps. Pop builds up the fire. Sandra is in the bathroom.

Sammy sits by the fireplace, his feet up. A glorious blaze. He promised to dazzle, has worse than failed. But it is a strange syndrome. He wonders how much of his life he will give to it. He has to make this decision, soon, for the Board as well as for himself. Dimmesdale could be a serious problem. Yet life is a lot more than fighting Dimmesdales. He wants that lot more, yes. He has tried for, gotten, given away a lot more. The research centre he started right our of med school, its grand successes quickly in lymph node immunology, getting the General to take it under its fiscal wing; soon, with luck, their own properly equipped building. Enough?

In the past he has often thought yes clearly enough. Enough for most any man to be satisfied with: public success, private happiness. Sandra. Before, Deirdre. A fabulous love, however brief. Love? Maybe the wrong word. What's the matter, Sam? Is replacing words something like losing them? What then? Infatuation? Only a few months long but the only time in his life of thorough bedazzlement. No question, he felt something immensely real. Or pieces of something real, Sammy? Aspects of Deirdre, your selected moments? And the drift, when did it begin? Other sides of her came clear, other parts. Sure those were always there, you just hadn't noticed. And so, months of projecting your first Deirdre onto the newly clear one, right? And now what? Projecting the old directorship onto the next six years, Sammy? What, its prestige? power? When is Deirdre no longer Deirdre? True, Sam has tried hard to be subtle, to understand his position clearly; has piled on descriptions: guiding directorship, insidious directorship; helpful, draining, protective, stress-filled, healing directorship. Underneath, has the job slithered into something else? When did your directorship stop being *your* directorship?

Sandra sits beside him, nestles against him. Silently they watch the fire.

Rosie unloads the dishwasher. Pop goes to wake Midgie.

They turn on the TV. Times Square is as ever. Everywhere the world changes. They count down. Much hugging, much kissing, a few discrete tears.

Midge will watch the Tournament of Roses parade with her father. And get to know Sandra better. Pop will drive Midgie over. "It looks as if Sandra is going to be a very big part of my life."

Pop tucks the covers around her. "We'll see. Sleep well, little Midgie." He strokes her hair.

She opens her eyes, grins.

He turns off the light. Growing up new even tonight, right under his nose.

Rosie's lamp is already off when Pop comes in. "You think they'll get married?"

"I don't know, Rosie, I just don't know. Can't call this one."

"Seems like there're all kinds of tensions there. Under the surface."

"Little ones, maybe."

Big enough, Rosie thinks.

Pop gets into his pyjamas, lies down, leans over, kisses her cheek. And under Rosie's surface?

They speak very little driving back.

Driving home . . . That, thinks Sandra, would be nice. A family. Since Tyke's father died— A home, Tyke and Sammy and her. Maybe even a baby, not really too late.

Too late to head off for the hospital for a few minutes? Probably. The hospital? You mean your office? or the lab? He feels Sandra lean against him, puts his arm around her. Protective, guiding, understanding. He could be any of these for her. And inspired, insightful, imaginative; seeing in his mind's eye the clear structures of the immune deficiency even before his evidence proves they are there: could he be that kind of researcher? Such a man would be called a, called (?)—for weeks he has not been able to find the word. He drives on, his outer speed unchanged. But he senses now some kind of internal change; and growing. To?

His apartment. They prepare for bed. Her manner has become sexual, she moves close, there are smiles, strokes, the negligee. He sees, responds; a kind of dream and feather touch of intercourse follows. She sleeps.

He is awake an hour; two; longer. The word, the kind of researcher, is not there. But he is realizing, very slowly, it is not there because there is no such word. Not in his language. In any language of the nations where the sciences of medicine are practised? He does not know, could not know. The kind of man he wants to be there are no nouns to label. This time he has not lost the label. It does not exist. Yet? Or any longer? What is under those nouns he has lost? Nouns, words altogether, that he uses to delimit his world: is he losing his ability to describe? Or—and he laughs with a bit of a shiver—is his world losing its ability to delimit his daily life? Are the nouns of his world—

He thinks then in another way: these names of things, did they long ago make him immune to that world? And, losing nouns, is he losing that immunity? Because if there is no label then mustn't he shift out from under the lost memory of its shell and find some other way to grasp what the label covers? Somehow?

Maybe cures for such dysphasia don't exist. But isn't there something good, essential sometimes, that certain immune systems should break down? Would you dare say that out loud, Sammy? For example at a conference, Sammy? He laughs lightly. Stop it, Sammy.

Health, the proper functioning of one's whole system. Of any system. Breakdown of health: when the system no longer can withstand the barraging stress of garbage from the world. The symptoms become visible then, they point out the illness within. And so *no*, this loss of nouns is no joke, Sammy. Don't treat is as a joke, Sammy, not ever. It could be a most important event, this loss. And here a dreadful paradox: what of those poor bastards with this acquired immune deficiency? Their most important event as well. Have you too lost the immunity that forces you to go on? Directorships, benefactors—

Eyes closed, not sleeping, his brain for a moment makes other shifts, other connections: airplane companies losing their immune systems, national embassies losing their immune systems, nuclear reactors losing— The immune system of the very social structure. People, machines, societies. Everyone, not only experts, seeing the diseases within.

Seeing, knowing; not responding. Immune to seeing and knowing? Lucy, burning. Tyke, rotting. Rosie—

The night-thoughts come and go, come again. Stay, settle in; neighbours, new associates. Sam watches night grey into morning. He hasn't slept. He isn't tired.

DEVILS

PER BRASK

From the back and ten or eleven meters off you didn't notice right away that there was something peculiar about the group of men who seemed to be posing for a photograph in the middle of the park. They all wore the same black, tight-fitting cut of suit. They were arranged around what from the back looked like a large chair. Two were standing on platforms at each side of the chair and the rest were either standing on the ground or sitting on benches in symmetrical groups, giving the chair focus in the picture.

If you moved slightly to the left or the right, however, so that you were at a sufficient angle to see the group in profile, not only would you notice the very young photographer, a boy who looked to be about nine or ten years old, but you would immediately see that the group of men he was taking a picture of were a group of no less than twelve devils.

If you are surprised reading this, you can well imagine my reaction as I kept moving to get a better, more frontal view of this sight. Curiously, fear never entered my mind, only fascination.

The devils, were not, of course, wearing the suits I thought I saw. They weren't wearing anything, in fact. As I moved towards a better angle I could see that they were all smiling, their black teeth shining in the sun and their horns held upright (I assumed, for a better composition in the photo).

Then the boy said: "Hold it, the light's not right."

All the devils relaxed their positions and gave expression to their disappointment in various groans and grunts. It was then that I saw the splendid one in the middle. He was bright orange-red with a few black markings. He sat straight with his legs crossed in front of him. Above him was a huge wooden mask of a devil with a golden rim. This beautiful carving was what I had taken from the back to be a large chair, which will give you a sense of its size.

"All right, here we go again," the boy called out. "Say, 'cheese.' "

"Cheese!" the devils responded. This was going to be a really fine picture.

After the picture the devils undid their symmetrical grouping, brought the mask down and stood around laughing and talking to one another.

I went over to speak to the boy.

"Hi," I said in a friendly and unthreatening manner knowing the sensitivity to strangers children are being taught today. The boy, however, seemed unfazed by my approach.

"Hi," he said.

"You certainly know how to construct a good image, young man."

"Thank you. I learnt it from my mother," the child said proudly.

"How did you get the idea for the devils?"

"Idea?"

"I mean, where did you get the costumes and the mask? School project?"

The boy just laughed and called the devils over. He introduced me to each one of them. They were all extremely friendly and happy to make my acquaintance, they said. Their handshakes were firm and all of them had very warm hands, almost hot, I'd say. It was soon clear to me that these gentlemen were not in costume, but that they were what they appeared to be, devils.

After pleasantries had been exchanged all twelve devils disappeared. They simply vanished, evaporated into thin air. The boy seemed unconcerned about this saying that he'd see them at dinner tonight as there was to be a party for the red devil whose nine hundredth birthday was today. Hence the photo with all his brothers.

"He is almost exactly a hundred times older than me," said the boy. "I turned nine nine days ago."

Aha, I said to myself, there we have it: *nine* hundred, *nine* years, *nine* days. Three nines in a row. Three upside-down sixes. How clever. When I mentioned this discovery to the boy he simply said, "You're very perceptive."

A brief silence followed. Then: "You're very lucky to be able to see them. Most people are not so privileged." And indeed, he was right because I suddenly recalled that several people who had walked past the group earlier had not made any signs of noticing them. And they certainly weren't normal.

I struck up a conversation with the boy whose name was Jacob. That's right. Jacob, the Hebrew name which means "the supplanter."

This may be an opportune time for me to mention that I am a

medievalist by profession and although necromancy and the black arts are not my field, I have taught a couple of courses where these matters were touched on tangentially. My excitement at this research opportunity is, thus, I think, understandable.

I walked with Jacob to a photo store with same-day service. He wanted to have his film developed before the evening's dinner party. When I mentioned my surprise that he expected his picture of the devils to come out, he told me that only people who were capable of seeing the devils in life would be able to see them in the photo.

On our way to the store I learnt a great many things from Jacob. First of all, I learnt that people's sensitivity to the presence of devils varied enormously. It had to do with chemical refractions of light on the eyeballs, so your ability to see them was dependent upon an exact pressure level in your eyeballs and had nothing to do with your moral standing. You could, however, like Jacob, be trained, via the black arts, to maintain this exact pressure.

As you must have perceived already, Jacob was not a normal child of nine. His language skills and his capacities for abstraction were much closer to those of a good university student in his senior year. Jacob explained that his mother had taught him since the age of three, and from the age of five he had been able to study necromancy on his own. He was uncertain how to explain his uncommon abilities, but he thought that the genetic mixture of his East-German mother and his Mexican father, combined with a life of continuous cultural crossovers (he and his mother had been living in Canada for the past four years) had made him disposed towards a highly developed understanding of human conduct, which is, after all, the basis for all other understanding. His mother, who had come to Mexico at the age of nineteen, (having met and married a Mexican official at the embassy in East Berlin) had involved herself so deeply in the Catholicism and the folklore of Michoacan (where she had moved with her husband) that as she progressed through the layers of belief and superstition she came out on the other side overwhelmed by the powers of darkness. For this Jacob felt eternally grateful. His mother had instantly started to teach him. She was now the high priestess of a coven right here in Winnipeg. Jacob's mother had only married his father to get out of the D.D.R., and when a favourable opportunity (another man, a tourist) presented itself, she and Jacob had packed up and left for more prosperous climes.

I also learnt why I might have been favoured with my first vision of devils. Jacob explained that particular day was unique in that it was a day when (within the lunar cycle which forms the basis for how devils record time) the red devil's birthday fell on the exact same day in the year as when he was born. Devils count only the birthdays in which the full lunar cycle begins anew. A year for a devil is therefore thirty-some of our years long and so the red devil was well past twenty-seven thousand years old today. Anyhow, given the lunar position of that particular day and perhaps some kind of subconscious intent on the part of the red devil, the pressure of my eyeballs had changed on that special day in that unique year.

After we had delivered the film at the store, and Jacob was about to go home, I let him subtly know that I would give much to be present at the evening's dinner party.

"Even your soul?" he asked.

I stiffened.

"Don't worry, we don't believe in that stuff any more," Jacob said, and laughed.

"You don't?"

"No. You are what you are. Your genetic structure makes you a flower, a cat, a devil or a human."

I knew what he meant by that, and after a little more humorous give-and-take, he gave me the address where the party was to take place and informed me that I needn't bring a present or anything else.

The address Jacob had given me was in the well-to-do suburb of Tuxedo, very close to the Assiniboine Park where I had met him earlier that day. The house was hidden behind some very large trees and as I approached it I looked for any signs of abnormality in design and colour. The house proved to be a normal, if large, white bungalow. I was to arrive at 7:06 p.m. (6:66 p.m., sic!) precisely, and as I was a couple of minutes early I took advantage of the impeccable sense of normalcy which exuded from the house to relax and collect my thoughts. At precisely the appointed time I rang the doorbell which activated the soothing suburban chimes. The door was opened and in front of me stood a very pretty woman evidently of Germanic origin. She had long, thick blonde hair and wore a bright red, loose cotton top and a flowing, long black skirt which fitted snugly around her slim waist. Her facial features were arranged to give the impression of gentle kindness and intelligence.

"Hullo," she said. "I am Jacob's mother, Bathsheba; you may call me Beth. We like to keep things informal here."

Bathsheba. I was thunderstruck. In Hebrew that name means "daughter of the oath." I introduced myself to her and she said that she already knew much more about me than I did myself.

I was let into a very large living room/dining room where the very tasteful furniture was almost overpowered by hundreds of bouquets of roses, black and red, side by side. Most of the devils were standing around the dinner table where a buffet had been laid out. Six black candles adorned the table. The plates were black, as were the napkins wrapped around golden cutlery. Some devils stood around the room with cocktail glasses and chatted. Jacob came over to me and said he was glad I could come. He took me around the room and the devils and I nodded in recognition of one another. The red devil said that he was particularly glad to see me, his birthdays were rarely attended by the uninitiated and it was a good sign that his Father (I don't know how to explain it but you could hear the capital "F") had willed it. I stated that I had come of my own volition which caused laughter amongst the seven or so devils within our reach. Their laughter was not malicious in any way. It sounded more like the kind of laughter parents make when their small child has said something accidentally amusing.

"You will soon learn," the red devil said.

Most of the evening passed uneventfully, as most dinner parties in suburbia: nothing much of importance being said or done, the occasional chat on current political affairs, but generally nothing more than your normal uncommitted and uncommitting jovial intercourse. The most interesting conversation I had was with Jacob and Beth who were willing to answer some of my questions and who did not produce gentle laughter at my curiosity.

From them I learnt that the reason why there was only one red devil was because devils turn red on their birthdays. The red and black roses were an important symbol for the devils as they are born (literally) out of red roses and very quickly thereafter turn black. The roses are to them symbols of both birth and life. The big mask I'd seen in the park, and which was also present in the room, was an artistic rendering of the face of the Father (again I swear I could hear the capital "F") of all devils, Satan himself. The devils felt very strongly about their family and they always carried their Father's portrait with them. Nobody could actually see Satan, not even the devils, but they knew that He (I could hear the capital "H") was always present, everywhere.

The only really unique event happened at 12:12:12 a.m. (double 6:66, sic!) when the red devil called out "My name is now Carl." The other devils started to clap in rhythmic beats producing a hollow but not eerie sound. Each time their hands met, more of the colour red disappeared from the now increasingly black devil. What earlier were only markings grew and grew to cover him. After six minutes he was as black as the rest of them.

When I asked Beth and Jacob what that little ritual was about, they told me that I had seen a nicknaming ceremony. Before a birthday-devil returns to black he must announce the name by which he is to be known till his next birthday. Devils do not have names, only nicknames, I was told. Apparently this is because their "hidden" names are so terrible that if uttered they could unleash horrible calamities. So those names were kept hidden until needed.

On my way home from the party I already began in my mind to compose the results of this research. In fact, I was so anxious to put everything down on paper that I began to write as soon as I arrived home.

The article I wrote that night is probably one of the finest pieces of scholarly writing I have ever committed. I have, however, by now received sixty-six rejection slips from decreasingly prestigious journals around the world. The problem with my article (which of course covers a greater territory, i.e., historical data and references to other research in the area, than I've needed to describe in this context) is that precisely those characteristics of the life of devils, which I've divulged here, I cannot substantiate with references to earlier research. I am the first researcher to have encountered the birthday ceremony of devils. My colleagues do not believe me. In fact, they are becoming increasingly unbearable in their disdain of my work and I fear that my credibility has suffered irreparably. It is for that reason only that I have finally stooped to presenting my findings in this unfortunate manner. But, the Truth will out.

V

ON THE QUEEN'S BIRTHDAY

PER BRASK

SKULL

GEORGE SZANTO

ON THE QUEEN'S BIRTHDAY

PER BRASK

Maybe it was only in my imagination but the light did appear very strange. When I qualify the statement like that it is because no one else seemed to take note of it, including my wife and our two small children. But it certainly seemed to me that there was something oddly violet about the light. Yet, of the group of about ten thousand people attending the change of the guards at the Amalienborg Castle to celebrate Queen Margrethe's forty-sixth birthday I was the only one looking up at the sky and not, like all the others, expectantly towards the balcony where the Queen, her prince and two sons were to appear minutes later.

The Amalienborg Castle in Copenhagen was built in the 1750s by King Frederik V. It comprises four palaces situated around a large square, two and two across from one another, two palaces situated on a north-south axis and two on an east-west axis. The buildings are in sandstone and are beautiful examples of rococo architecture. In the centre of the square, a bronze statue of Frederik built in 1764 by J.B. Saly creates a curious sight in this northern climate as the king, on his horse, sits clad as a Roman emperor wearing garlands, cape and sandals.

The green, oxidized copper roofs, the manifestation of an eighteenth century Danish king's fantasies of empire and the strange, even "wrong," light of the day combined to produce in me a feeling of utter disbelief in the reality around me. Had it not been for the fact that my four-year-old son, who was sitting on my shoulders in order to get a view of the impressive guards in red uniforms and black bearskin hats, pulled my hair in an attempt to gain better balance, I would have thought I was dreaming. I felt out of it, as if I were having a physiological reaction to an aesthetic phenomenon.

I attempted to bring my wife's attention to what I was seeing but the noise of the crowd drowned my voice despite the fact that she and our eight-year-old daughter were standing but twenty-five feet away, their gazes fixed at the balcony as the Queen came out.

The multitude roared, greeting their sovereign with an enthusiasm I'd come to believe was impossible in our time.

Despite my son's protestations and his tearing at my hair I moved out of the crowd to stand a little out of the way for a better perspective on the scene. He calmed quickly, however, as he joined the crowd in yelling the traditional nine hurrahs for Denmark and waving his little Danish flag, occasionally into my eyes. He was clearly mesmerized participating in this little yearly ritual. We'd taken our daughter to Denmark before but this was his first time, visiting his grandparents and seeing some of his heritage on his father's side.

As I turned to scratch my face, which had grown prickly in the wind, my son pulled my face back and I noticed a little man to the left of us, about fifteen yards away, also standing behind the crowd. I freed my face from my son's hands and positioned him on my shoulders so he could look straight ahead and I could look at the little man dressed in a blue coat. When I say little, I mean that he couldn't have been much above four feet tall. Yet he was not a dwarf, just a small man. Apart from his size he was distinguished by curiously low cheekbones and a bald head which gave a severity to his expression. A large Hasselblad camera reached down to his chest. He was obviously standing behind the crowd in order to be able to take a photo of the Queen. He was working the camera with some difficulty, moving in a sort of ritualistic dance and when he finally pressed the trigger I felt as if time stood still momentarily. The crowd and the royal assembly froze. Then I saw the strangest sight.

Out of his camera emerged a replica of the Queen which travelled directly to the balcony and stood there while the Queen herself travelled from the balcony and into the camera. The whole operation was very rapid. Everyone except I seemed frozen. My son sat still on my shoulder, even the flag which he held in front of my face was stiff and unmoving in suspended reality. I saw the exchange take place, but I was unable to move. When the event was completed the crowd continued as before while the new, but exact replica, Queen waved her hand and went into her palace with her family.

I started to move towards the little man and as he noticed me I could see fear in his eyes and his mouth clearly forming the words "Oh, no." Then he ran. I rushed my son over to my wife and without any explanation I set off after the little man telling my family to "wait for me here." As I turned to run I saw him turn down a major street which I knew would soon be crowded with the Queen's well-wishers so I set off with greater speed than I thought myself capable of. As I came to the corner of the street I stopped to check my bearings and to see if I could catch a glimpse of the little man. I saw him nowhere. However, after a few moments of letting my eyes search the street I noticed a Hasselblad camera sticking out from an alcove at a candy shop. He was obviously expecting to be able to hide till the multitude would enter the street and then disappear in the crowd. In order to fool him I crossed the road and started to "search" down the street almost perpendicular to his hiding place. Then I disappeared around a corner from whence I could follow his every move. By now the streets around the castle were filled with people but I had gotten myself into position just in time. Obviously feeling secure that his strategy had worked the little man finally came out of hiding and walked nonchalantly down the street. I followed him and got up to a fairly close range as he walked into a building. I hurried into the building in time to see the basement door close. Quietly, I slipped down the steps, opened the door and found myself in a dark and damp basement. My own breath silently echoed in the hall, and I realized how fast I had run earlier. I dared not light a match nor search for a lightswitch, but as my eyes grew accustomed to the dark I could faintly see a row of doors and a slight line of light appearing from one of them. I went to that door and I could hear someone humming in there. Though I had never heard the little man's voice before I knew that this was his.

I swung open the door and entered a small room filled with strange objects: masks, hats, goat heads carved in wood, coloured sticks, and, on the far wall, a strange pattern painted in gold. This was not a normal residence. The little man stood quietly in the middle of the room, not knowing what to do since I was blocking his only possible escape. Then he said to me in English, "Can I help you?"

"I speak Danish," I answered.

"I don't," followed his short reply, and added, "Can I help you?" this time slightly irritated.

"What happened back there?"

"Back where?"

"Don't be foolish, I saw you replace Queen Margrethe with, with . . . Queen Margrethe."

There was a brief silence during which he relaxed and then said, "I was afraid you might. Don't worry, nothing happened."

"What do you mean?" I exclaimed. "I saw it with my own eyes."

He sighed, "I don't know how you could. No one has ever been able to see it. But I promise you it was completely harmless. Nothing has changed. Nothing will change by it. Would you like some tea?"

"I don't understand," I said.

"I'm not surprised. Would you like some tea?"

I didn't answer him but kept my guard at the door.

"Don't worry," he said, "I won't run. Besides, no one would ever believe you if you told them. Come, have a seat. I've got some great tea in my thermos."

I hesitated a moment, then left my post at the door which closed behind me as I sat in the appointed chair.

"What happened?" I repeated.

"Nothing," he said. "You simply witnessed Merlin's jolly vindictiveness."

"What?" I laughed.

"Merlin has punished me. Condemned me to pursue ineffective magic for an undetermined length of time."

In response to my expression of disbelief he continued, "I am an apprentice of Merlin's. I travel through time. We can do that you know, but the prerequisite is that we are not allowed to influence things because that will change the course of history. Now, I did that once, influenced things, and for that Merlin has condemned me to travel around and do the kind of thing you observed me doing today. I do magic but it doesn't affect anything. When Merlin feels I've done it for long enough he'll bring me back to our time and release me from his little joke."

The tiny man told me that he had done his little "trick" on all the prettiest queens and princesses of Europe. Besides Queen Margrethe he had "replaced" Queen Silvia of Sweden, Princess Diana of England, Queen Beatrix of Holland and Princess Paola of Belgium, all with absolutely no effect, of course. His particular penchant for queens and princesses he explained as a simple question of homesickness.

After a while I felt that we were sufficiently at ease for me to ask him about his crime. At first he would not talk about it, but after a little prompting he started: "Merlin and I were out time-travelling together through the nineteenth century and it was clear to me that things in that century were going terribly wrong, the human imagination which had conceived of great things seemed to me to begin to rot, machines were starting to become masters, grimness and dullness were shooting their deep roots into the human soul, that sort of thing. I asked Merlin if I could study the situation a little more in depth which he agreed to let me do. When he had left, however, I felt I had to do something. I knew I wasn't allowed so I had to hatch an extremely subtle plot. This is what I did: I travelled to the year 1829 in the Alhambra Castle in Granada, a gorgeous red construction built in sections between 900 and 1492 by the Moors. I knew that an American author by the name of Washington Irving was staying there trying to get inspiration for a book. I disguised myself as a servant and offered my services to him. I took the name Matteo Ximenes, pretended my family's roots went far into the Moorish past, and I then fed him the wondrous stories he was later to become famous for. That way I managed to stave off the advent of Naturalism by some forty years. Industrialized mankind could dream just a little longer. Merlin discovered my efforts, of course, and decided to punish me, as I've told you."

I was completely flabbergasted by the little man's story and starting to feel a little dizzy. I mentioned it to him, and he said that in order not to be punished again he had put a little powder in my tea which would make me question the reality of our conversation very soon.

I told him that I might write down my experiences of the day, to which he said: "You're welcome to do so, but I must warn you that your statements will appear not only to others but also to yourself as a fiction, and one without effect, for things have changed drastically since my little experiment."

For the past half hour I've been writing this down on twelve serviettes in a little cafe around the corner. I've tried to recast my experience into sentences but they just won't capture the reality of my encounter with Merlin's apprentice. The words slip and slide into a story; and I'm sliding with them. . .

SKULL

GEORGE SZANTO

> Wounded Knee, South Dakota— Some 250 members of the militant American Indian Movement seized the trading post and church in this historic hamlet on the Oglala Sioux reservation today. The insurgents are demanding that the U.S. Senate Foreign Relations Committee hold hearings on all treaties made with Indians, and that the Senate start a "full-scale investigation" of the government treatment of Indians.
>
> —*Montreal Star*, Feb. 28, 1974

Claire had bought the skull more than a year ago. Against her better judgement, but there it was. The elaborate carving on the jawbones and high cheeks fascinate her, still now. A woman's skull, the peddler had said. Seven hundred years old, easy.

It sits on her desk at home, staring directly. She managed to get it all the way back unbroken, unscathed, which pleased her. Then she didn't know what to do with it, so set it down on the desk till she could decide. There it stays, variously a paperweight and sometime interlocutor.

Somebody, maybe Teddy playfully or Web if he is in one of his ironic *memento mori* moods, always seems to turn the thing so its empty sockets will catch Claire's eye at the least glance up from her work. Not an unfriendly or frightening stare; scrutiny, rather. As if it wants to know everything about me, Claire had said. Last week the thought came to her, *Maybe now it does.* Which has, moments ago, led on to: *If only it could say.*

They are home, mid-afternoon Sunday, because of the quarrel this morning down in Vermont. Like all their arguments it was over trivia. *Watch Claire follow it through in her mind.*

Outside the sky had been blue, newly spotted with clouds. Teddy had pulled on his cross-country boots. The cottage has thick curtains, well-lined. At home here in Montreal their drapes are worn. Claire feeling the heft of those there in the rented place had decided: "I'll remake the curtains in the front room."

"The what?"

"The curtains. At home. Reline them." Making the offer she felt a keen pleasure, a generosity.

Web had glanced over as if not understanding. "What for?"

"They'll be warmer. Look better."

"You know how much time that'll take?"

"I'll spread it out, I don't know—a few weeks."

"Months you mean."

"I'm perfectly capable of redoing a couple of curtains."

"Claire. You start in on these curtains, we might as well give up skiing this winter. Okay? Or maybe you can stay in town and Teddy and I'll go skiing. You stay home and stitch? Don't be absurd."

Teddy had put on his jacket. He went outside.

"I am hardly absurd. I—"

"We can buy new ones, okay? I've never much liked those yellow things anyway. Come on Claire—"

Next thing he'd say, Don't be ridiculous. She had waited, felt her approaching withdrawal—

"Really, Claire, be smart."

—and everything good between them, the morning, the cottage, skiing, the ease, she had watched it spiral off, grow grey, fade . . .

Should she believe he is right? She does dislike being domestic when the task goes on and on. But the idea of buying something new if there is still life and use in the old, this she finds hard to deal with. Claire, raised not to waste, thinks often of thrift. Her mother had known how to cope, elegantly even, with the old. But quickly such a notion seems part of another century. Claire now and then feels she doesn't belong to her own time. Or figures she ought to be, today, sixty-five instead of half that. Retired and done.

This late afternoon she has a headache. Probably from their excess of last night, whiskey sours, the wine. Shouldn't have opened the second bottle, not for only two. Still it was a good evening, good talk. Teddy had skied all day and was asleep by seven-thirty. Claire and Web had taken the chance to catch up on the week: the two new books she has accepted—she is an associate editor at Davis and Lebrun, Montreal's largest English-language publishing house—one on Canada's role in the Vietnam war, another on cold weather gardening; he elaborated the newest wrinkles on three internecine squabbles in his department at the university; funny stories, fascinating. Web is hilarious when vindictive. Good shared talk. They had drifted on to directions they might guide Teddy in: let him get serious about his piano? A heck of a way to make a living, ultimately. His photography was getting better by the month, what to do there? But it's the kind of thing kids outgrow . . .

This afternoon, back in Montreal, thinking about last night, the headache gets worse.

It has grown out of the argument, one of many of a sort; simple, typical. She, while in it, had watched it, as she sees it now, follow almost the path of the big one last summer: which of the Vermont houses they'd narrowed their search down to did they really want to rent. That is, she thought they'd narrowed down. But Web had, already beyond discussion, decided.

This choice between possible skiing bases had itself been only the final stage in a larger give-and-take: should they rent in Vermont at all or stay in the Eastern Townships. Web had insisted on Vermont: far greater choice of hills, their dollar went farther, by and large better snow and clearer weather. The Townships seemed pretty good to her, people there they knew, not so far. Besides, Vermont meant a hassle twice a weekend, Web still an American and the border buzzing with draft dodger checks. Landed immigrant status was a category customs authorities on both sides had to use their intelligence to deal with and how many times had Web said those guys are put on the border exactly because they're brainless. In the end he won the first part of the argument because Vermont is pretty and she didn't want to demean the discussion with stupid suggestions of jingoism. On either side.

The two Vermont places, each available for minimum six months, November through April, were opposites—the one an old farmhouse off a dirt road, perfect for both cross-country right there at the door and for alpine, Stowe eleven miles away; the other a little two-bedroom ranch-type, snug and sealed.

Web loved it. At the end of August he'd said, "Claire, this little place, it'd be easy to care for, no problems."

"Yes but we want to be in the country." The ranch place was in an area that came close to suburban, a medium-sized development.

"Who knows if they even plow that dirt road."

"I asked. They do."

"It's a lot easier to get to the little place."

"Come on. It'd be fun to live in a farmhouse."

They'd asked Teddy. He carefully backed away: "Both places are great, I think." He'd taken pictures of each. The shots did make both houses look good.

Claire had let herself be convinced mostly by Web's argument-from-simplicity: Sunday evening we just lock up the place and there's nothing to worry about till next Friday. While who knows what can go wrong with a hundred-year-old farmhouse?

Even then she tried to resist: "But the landlord's responsible—"

"And if he doesn't show up? Or care?"

Deep-down she knew the farmhouse would have been okay, great even. But she couldn't locate the way to say this. "The farmhouse makes me feel more like I want to ski." The best she could find.

No Claire, you have to look deeper yet. . . .

"Listen, let's not be stupid, if we're going to have to sit in Montreal and worry about somebody breaking into a deserted farmhouse or worry about the roof collapsing under the weight of the snow we won't get any pleasure out of this winter at all."

When their give-and-takes descend to about here her head starts to hurt. In early September, Claire had acquiesced.

The curtains argument had taken the pleasure out of more skiing this morning. Now she sits at her desk and stares at the skull. Outside it is almost dark. The skull stares back. Why do she and Web argue exactly like this, beginning lightly, suddenly each sticking to principles so deeply buried they could've been as ancient as the skull itself? She plays with these questions sometimes.

All possible answers lie buried in murk. She draws the skull to her, strokes its cheekbones—high like her own; how much does she really identify with it? She imagines how flesh and skin would have formed a face over the bone. It is a kind of ritual with her, this ongoing projection. She looks into the open eyeholes as if trying to find the spirit within. Who had this woman been? She cradles the cranium in two hands. With her right palm she presses, gently. There, back there, was her headache.

Look, the peddler had told her, see the high cheekbones. Very unusual among the Mixtecs, unknown even. Yet it was found not twenty kilometres from here. She must have been very beautiful. If he may say, cheekbones like the señora's own.

A week from now she will write a poem about some of this. She has been working on a book of poems for over a year. She wished she had enough time for her writing. There is a novel in her, two maybe. She reads piles of manuscripts and could do better herself, a lot. But where to find the time. One day maybe.

With a fingernail she traces the carved lines on the skull. The peddler had said it came from a long-covered tomb. The woman herself hadn't been buried there, it wasn't the grave of a woman at all. A Mixtec king had been lain to rest there, or at least a great general, her skull boiled, the flesh peeled off, the bones dried and worked with carvings, the lovely ornament placed by the king's head to please him forever.

Claire had thought but not said: Either you are lying about the age of it in which case why should I buy this thing. Or you are committing a crime, you are selling off a piece of Mexico's heritage, you are selling your patrimony. True, the carving on the chin had intrigued her, two Quetzalcóatls, feathered serpents, tiny, beginning at the back of the jaw there where the ears would have been, two snake-heads meeting below the two front teeth. Was Quetzalcóatl Mixtec? The snakes had disgusted her at first; she feigned disinterest, turned away. But this immediate too easy reaction had irritated her. She'd turned again, to stare. It seemed to draw her in. What could she do with such a thing? She wishes Web had been with her; to say, sensibly, Come on, don't be silly, let's go, lots more of this Monte Albán place still to see. But Web was in Montreal and the peddler, her fascination his entry, had followed Claire for nearly ten minutes. She gave in, eight dollars and it was hers. Just to get rid of him she told herself. It'd be a present for Web when she got back, a souvenir. At customs in Montreal she didn't declare it. Unpacking, she knew Web would find it absurd. She gave him a silver belt buckle instead, her fall-back present.

It was then she set it on her desk. Was she completely wrong, did the skull look pleased to be sitting here? Better here than stuck away in some box of her husband's. In his drawer or whatever it might've had a little privacy, but—

Much happier here.

The trip to Mexico: she had gone on her own, had been wanting to see the ancient non-European cultures for years. Web too always said he'd like to, really, one day. But she'd come to realize he wouldn't ever, none of that interested him in the least, oh he might go along to be with her but that was all. A waste of money therefore. In Mexico she took the time at last to think herself through. A bit of herself anyway, she'd never been much given to introspection and hated shrinks and despised at least a little all those people who spent time and money that way.

Claire Homeson née Silver. Thirty-three, a respectable editor, married twelve years, well-educated, reasonably happy, distressed these days by the political actions of her adopted homeland the U.S., on a week's holiday had discovered she wanted to work not simply on other people's books but to bring her own into existence; words, images. The day she bought the skull she wrote her first poem. In the year since then it has been revised two dozen times anyway. She is still not satisfied. Even stuck in her drawer it reaches up to her, through wood and blotter, to visibility.

Street Scene, Mexico 1973

Dead dog,
ten thousand flies,
people standing round
paying no attention;
barely worth a mention.
Except a boy has found a stick,
whips the ground,
brown dust flies,
thick around the dog.
Half covers it.

It will go through yet more revisions. She said last week to her friend the skull: Maybe even a vision. It distresses her sometimes, as now this Sunday afternoon, the dark gathering, that she cannot see the real face the woman once had. No features take form in Claire's mind, no specific image. But right away she chides herself for this lazy thinking: of course there is an image. Each time. Trouble is, each time it's different. Claire often hates this as much in the skull as in herself, this inconsistency. Chin, how? Cheeks, how? Brow, how? She has taken to repeating these words, no more than an intake of breath really, as she wonders. A small ritual gesture. Weak, formless; unproductive?

Where this thought has come from she can have no idea yet. *The skull's seven-hundred-year perspective—*

Teddy—the Leica was the birthday present he wanted, none of those new Japanese cameras for him, both sets of grandparents had contributed—took a series of pictures of the skull. In broad daylight or as shadows crept across it, in the dark with a flash, with overhead light and time exposure, at all times the skull stared out. Not that every photo was full-face; yet the thing watched you however you looked at each picture. "Mum? Why d'you think that is?

"It's strange." Always staring. And always a different face on the skull. Changes, unperceived in the process, pure and clear in the skull or its picture. Eerie. Never calling for fear, though. "Maybe your lighting?"

Teddy had doubted this. But given to experiment anyway he agreed it'd be worth shooting the skull in the wrong light, at a bad angle like say from behind or into the ear cavity. Naturally in those shots she could see nothing was staring out at her. But—and here she admitted her imagination was working overtime—it felt as if the thing was watching nonetheless, still understood what she was all about. As if it watched through a mirror or a reflection in a window. Neither of which appeared in the photos though these, two small windows, a floor-length mirror, are in the room. As if the skull has a sense of humour all its own, and a vindictiveness, gentle yet dominant. Something like Web, talking about his associates at the university: the amazing complexes of human foibles; and his ability to understand such complexity from the outside. This kind of perception gives Web an immense measure of self-control, some armour protecting him from the worst absurdities of the world he functions in daily, and so a bit of breathing space. What need has a skull for self-protection, for space?

She is asking herself many more questions these days. Good.

The skull has a place of its own now, doesn't exist only to hold her papers down, is treated with the respect due a woman who has endured her place, bodiless, mind boiled away, beside a king or a great general. The new notion slithers again into Claire's mind: does it understand my past as well as my present? Brow, how? What wisdom was once up there? And—Claire shivers—as long as we're being a little perverse, getting rid of our humanoid barriers between life and death, between long ago and now, why not also abolish the invisible line between now and tomorrow, next week, 1978, 1987? How, chin? Because suddenly the snakes there seem to wiggle precisely toward the future. Through the mouth, behind the teeth, there is where the future lies. Claire reaches over, picks it up again, brings the bone close to her face, feels the snakes with her eyes, touches the teeth one by one. In there? She feels a bit foolish. So what.

Protected, too; as by the skull? Here in her study while the world goes past outside? In Vermont in the cottage, oblivious to organized military murder half the globe away even as they ski with pleasure in the oppressor's country? Protected in summer at the place they'd taken last year on Lake Champlain while a president's goons broke into a Washington hotel? Absurd; yet it happened. Now she sits here, staring into the mouth of a skull.

She is not any kind of political activist. She marches when necessary and signs petitions. She and Web had come to Canada in 1968, she returning, they arriving together for his job though she likes to think they made that job happen because of the war, the U.S. becoming a bad place to bring up a kid. They had met in San Francisco, she there because, yes, she too was enamoured by the U.S. At least had been once. It still isn't a despicable nation she prefers to think. Just some corrupt leaders. True, consistently re-elected, as if they had some malignant magnetism. Or understood the social and domestic workings of their people so well as to be in control almost by magic, demonically. She sets the skull down, trying again not to ask about the future: Cheeks, how . . .

She stares out the window. The dark is now there, in streetlamp glare, behind whispers of blowing snow. A knock on her door.

Web: "I just called across the street to see if Carrie's free to baby-sit. We could go out for supper if we'd like."

Till asked she didn't know she wanted to. "Great."

They talk through the recurrent question, Where? He has a notion of a new Italian place across town, she likes the Greek restaurant around the corner.

"Come on, we always go there."

"Sure, because we love it."

"This place is supposed to be really good."

"Yeah but we'd have to drive." She looks out the window to dramatize her point. The snow whirls more thickly. "It could be a blizzard."

"We're tough."

"So let's walk."

Web starts to answer, decides not, shrugs. "Okay."

It is obvious to both this might have grown into precisely the kind of argument their quiet dinner is supposed to atone for. They leave. The evening does them good.

They are home by nine because of Carrie; tomorrow is school; Web walks her across the street.

Claire is back in her study. She needs to prepare some materials for the office, background on the Canadian content of all books they have brought out recently, the last five years. There is a take-over bid in the works. Wright and Dempsey Publishers in New York needs a Canadian outlet. All editors have to supply the newly constituted legal team with ammunition to fight W & D. Solid enough to stand up in court if necessary. Claire is opposed to the take-over possibility both in principle and because she likes her job just as it is. Confident in her opposition but not adamant, not as fanatic as are her three co-editors. Last week she'd tried out the argument-from-moderation: "It wouldn't be great but probably we could live with it, in fact W & D could give our books much larger U.S. distribution." The others practically tore her apart. It came down, finally, to her having been brainwashed because she'd lived in California for eight years, was therefore blind to the dangers of American ownership; management was domination. No she wasn't blind, she was trying hard to build in a little perspective, not easy, there were after all some good things about the U.S. too— Which they wouldn't give her leave to explain, irrelevant to the take-over bid.

These images move about in her brain as she selects the material to take along tomorrow. Each time she looks up the skull is watching. Reading her mind? Does it know how much she hates this whole backgrounding work, digging through files, legitimating decisions made in her earliest days on the job when she was functioning on pure instinct? Good work back then, coming from her own insight, without obvious rules. She doesn't know, now, which set of restraints she would dislike more: the proposed guidelines for Canadian content that if the ploy worked would keep them out of W & D clutches, or whatever W & D might impose on them if their lawyers failed. Does the skull know all this?

She is wondering such things now.

She likes the U.S., she admits it. Vermont and New Hampshire and Upper New York State anyway. The hills are good and old and rolling, the fields have been farmed for a couple of centuries plus, still keep producing wonderful corn and tomatoes, healthy pine and maple and so on. For the summer it was her argument that won out so they have gone back to the same place on Lake Champlain for three years, have just taken it for a fourth summer. Another act not approved of by her fellow editors. Web would have preferred to head into northern Quebec, find waters that were, in his joke, "almost virgin." He fishes, is serious about fishing, for him Champlain is fished out. Though he still gets his share of pike, bass and the occasional unlucky lake trout.

Their cottage sits at the water's edge. There Claire can lie in the hammock on the screened-in porch, watch all movement in front of her, speculate. And make notes. Some of these notes have turned into poems. Here is her favourite Lake Champlain poem:

History: Years from Now

A constant dance of dragonflies
Sweeping across flat evening water
Black wings against grey surface and a slate sky.
Destroyed
By images of helicopter battle:
Swoops of fire on a TV screen.
Why watch the present dance?

It must be asked
In another way: are dragonflies aware
Of our history?
The question is more metaphoric
Than it may sound: will we remember

The helicopter dance
Six hundred years from now?

She feels the verses catch some of her ambivalence, her state of mind these days, nearly spring 1974.

They do. But she can versify better. Will.

The attaché case is packed, only a night's sleep now between her and heading off. At the end of the hall Web is watching some movie on TV. She leans back in her chair. It was a good meal. Web had conceded this too. He always does, he loves Greek food. They had talked about the argument over the curtains, tried successfully not to relive it, pretty quickly its echoes died away. Because the skull had come back to her mind: how briefly the woman would have lived before being lain to sleep for what ought to have been forever beside the general or the king. Relining. Ridiculous.

Claire wonders what their old curtains can be used for. If they had a cottage of their own, on a lake say and usable too in the winter for skiing, they could have taken the old curtains out, put them on the windows there to block the winter wind creeping in through the cracks. A country nest to feather would be nice, one of their own, good to keep coming back to. But Web says he doesn't want to buy, he likes the flexibility of different places every year. Though he did accede to the Champlain cottage again. Were they growing closer in at least some of their notions? Or maybe just older. Web anyway. Claire smiles at this. And does not mind her friend smiling with her.

After the argument's tatters and shreds disappeared they talked about her, the time she needed, the novel that had to come out. He took her hand across the table. They interlaced their fingers beside the taramasalata, laughed at their ethnically-accented ongoing easy romance. "But seriously Claire, do quit. You don't need to work."

But the job is an independence for her, a world of her own. She is clear on this. Independence from? The house, Web, Teddy, the parts of life she loves?

Yes, and more, you know that too. Because at the same time, a dependence: mostly you need the job, don't you. The way a smoker craves her cigarette, a junkie his reprieve.

She is hooked on independence! She has not realized this till right now, this precise moment.

Web had gone on: "We can live on my salary, course we can. Maybe a little frugally, not a lot of dinners like this, so casually decided, but really what's more important than your freedom to do your own work?"

He was right, certainly—

Later in the meal, the bottle of wine empty (two days in a row; you shouldn't have, Claire), Web set it out, a formal if corny offer with the last sip in his glass: "Come on. I hereby give you time. You can do with it what you want. Live it in any way you want. I hereby give you freedom."

My husband is good, kind, generous: this thought slides now through her mind. But it is an uneven slide, a kind of rumpled slide. On and on it slithers sometimes easily sometimes clumsily around strange obstacles in the brain: he gives me everything I need, including time. Time to be by myself. Time for my own work. Time the most precious commodity. My time. The thought should make her glow warmly (or would it be the wine?) except there is an edge to it, sharp, even ragged, which makes no sense. Ragged edges slide badly.

A couple of years ago there was an argument over her going to Toronto for a few days. These images can come up from her memory now; not stored deep they are practically visible.

She knew she should go to the conference. The major publishers would be there. She'd meet people who till then were only voices on the phone. She could contribute on a couple of important questions. But Teddy had a messy cold, a touch of bronchitis maybe. Web had urged her, go nonetheless. "Of course you should. Come on, Teddy's fine with me, you don't think I can judge how he's feeling? Claire, please." Had he been giving her, then too, a kind of freedom? But she chose family responsibility: "No. I'll go next year." She nursed Teddy all weekend. He got neither better nor worse. The conference was to start Monday morning. At five Sunday evening she opened the closet and took out a suitcase.

"Where you going?"

"Toronto. The conference."

"Now?"

"Sure."

It was raining out, drizzling. "Have a reservation?"

"For what?"

"Plane, train? Hotel?"

"I'm driving." She grinned. He told her later it was the most impish, the worst impudent grin he'd ever seen.

"Into the night? The rain? Come on. Six hours? By yourself?"

She was not a strong driver, she knew that. "Yep."

This was completely indecipherable. "Claire, for petesake—"

"Just keep Teddy in bed. He'll be okay. I'll call tomorrow night."

She gave him a perfunctory hug. He didn't respond. More of the same smile, took the keys, strode out the door, felt her insurgence as a glow.

Web had been very angry. He had no clues, what had prompted this? Why such a departure, such arbitrary insistence?

Now she turns on a radio, the ten o'clock news. The story from Wounded Knee, South Dakota, puts everything else in the background. She listens with growing interest as a senator speaks of the implications of such action, intones rancour, outlines measures for removing the AIM leaders from the trading post. "There may be bloodshed." How had they reached this point, this militance? After this the rest of the news is boring. Because the headache is back? She will have to stop drinking wine. At thirty-three?

Maybe she'd only take a leave of absence, see if she actually could work alone, self-sustained and self-motivated. It would be a kind of halfway measure: Claire Homeson, half writer. She wonders how that role would suit her. Change her psychic, even her physical, appearance? Why not. She could have lots of appearances. Yes, she likes that notion. She looks in the mirror, wrinkles her brow, feels wise and thoughtful, strokes her chin to reinforce the image, its feeling. She relaxes her face, not a bad face, eyes and cheeks in good balance. Is this what Web sees? She giggles silently. Nice high cheekbones, the skull's like the señora's own. Okay. She sits again, stares at her friend, into her eyes. Leans forward, touches the cheeks, smoothes them.

A *sweet stroke*.

She runs her finger round each eye orifice. She has caught a touch of *memento mori* irony too. She leans back, sets the skull on her lap, muses calmly. Outside the window snow whirls softly. Where the woman with the carved chin comes from the sun shines all March long. In between here and there lies a nation, powerful, that says it has no desire to destroy. Claire believes this sometimes. Yet the destruction happens, beyond the wish. The skull looks up at her.

It is an evening made for clear thoughts. She knows this because she knows another has just shaped itself. Web has offered her time: time for herself, time to work. But, surely, time is not Web's to give. Where does Web get future time from, to hand down to her?

She will have to consider this. Carefully. At a slower speed. In her—she smiles—own time. Gently she sets the skull on the desk. And, not resisting an impulse, kisses it gently on the cheek.

Slowly she gets up, as if in a dream. Silently she puts the light out, opens the door, goes out. Quietly the room goes dark.

A dark room can be a relief also. Responsibility for Claire is weighty. But she's going to be okay. I'm sure of it.

VI

FERRY

GEORGE SZANTO

SEEKING THE BOTTOM, AGAIN

PER BRASK

FERRY

GEORGE SZANTO

The rusting car ferry brought him through the fog from North Sydney to Newfoundland. The air was a globe of slate. If he were fishing this water the mysteries below the surface would fascinate him. Now it was a trip with other ends. A sixteen hour crossing, begun at midnight, over the strait, past invisible outports. The ferry slowed, finally docked. His Oldsmobile, awkwardly positioned along the starboard wall at the rear of the lower deck, would be the last to disembark.

No. Another car. Two rows over, up by the exit port, humanless, a pickup waited, a solitary Datsun. He had heard, minutes before, much squawking of horns and some shouts. He'd paid no heed. Now he took the silent truck as explanation.

Where was the owner? Had he fallen sick, was he lying down? Asleep? Unconscious? Simply unaware of or indifferent to their regained contact with land. Perhaps locked by some freak accident in a toilet stall, or secreted in an emergency closet among life jackets and inflatable dories. Hiding from—? A mafioso trailing him, unpaid gambling debts. The RCMP, for embezzlement. His colourful, or colourless, past. His wife— Or was the pickup abandoned by a woman, or was the driver dead? So many causes, each a possibility.

The Olds drove by the Datsun. He felt a precipitous desire, a kind of imperative, to look inside, check the seats, the glove compartment, what about suitcases? Some clue to gender or history, intention, some link. A way to explain. One time only. Yes, as dramatic as that. But the line of cars moved along, rolling obediently onto shore.

He saw him then, just ahead, at the edge of the fog. How did he know who this was? The man, short but powerful, wore a light-coloured jacket. A black satchel hung by a strap from his shoulder. He carried a slender round case, as for fishing rods. From these details alone— He reached him, slowed, rolled a few yards beyond, stopped, slid over to the passenger seat to open the window, offer a ride. The man caught his gesture and turned away sharply.

Very well, he wouldn't interfere. The response, while abrupt, had not been inappropriate. Through the passenger-side mirror he found the man's image, outlined against afternoon grey, the least unified face he had ever seen. A group of features, out of control, eyes filled with sadness, traces of anger, a skin so white its pallor blared, hair thin and curly on top, on the sides angling out straight like a cat, spooked, undecided whether to run or fight.

A glimpse, nothing more. He re-entered the traffic. The fog, the line of cars, enforced a creeping pace. He searched for the man in the rear-view mirror. He thought he found a dash of white. In the fog it dimmed to invisibility.

Next morning, sunny, at breakfast miles away in the hotel in St. Johns, the radio a hum of voices, he caught at the end of the news a mention of a car abandoned on a ferry. The police were investigating.

He sipped his tea. They would know the licence plate, easy to track the man down. Computers, telephones, credit card controls, portable modem link-ups—

He studied his files, background for today's project, half his mind far away. How hard was it to disappear?

His business here could prove complex. He forced the ferry incident away. He had to meet them at their offices.

The day filled quickly with frustration and misunderstandings. He could not tell if his explanations were inadequate or if his counterparts were slow. In the evening he found no relief in food, wine, the television.

The front page of the morning paper, down at the bottom, pictured the face. A poor likeness, as from a passport or a driver's licence. Curls and lank hair both, here lying flat, were longer, a caricature. Whoever should see this man, Jeremy Turner, please inform the police.

He wondered if that meant him. He'd had no more than the momentary glimpse, and through a mirror at that. Surely the authorities had searched the boat, knew he was ashore. Would they think he'd jumped at sea? Besides, from the single glance, that terror of discovery, he felt no desire to give the man away. (Probably some would see this attitude as incorrect: irresponsible behaviour.) What did it matter. The man wanted, for his own reason, to remain apart.

He reflected on this for a minute or more, weighing its legitimacy. Then let it pass. Another full day lay ahead. Had the Newfoundland contract been wrong to try for? He shouldn't be involved. Then he thought: in a real sense he wasn't. The discovery made him laugh aloud. No wonder the situation seemed ready, increasingly, to dissolve on him.

Then through the laughter he caught his own paradox the more strongly. He would of course turn the project into a challenge. He always had. For a moment he pondered: what new ones lay ahead?

He drove to the meeting, comfortably alone in his Olds. He despised rental autos, like he hated flying. His own car was a place to think, to plan. Over the years he'd woven many a net of strategies there behind the wheel.

The morning went brilliantly. Not as a result of new bluffs, new compromises. No, he'd laid the groundwork the day before as was his practice, his habitual way. They had needed the night to consult among themselves. His deal was struck by noon.

It left a bad taste. All had gone well because he was good at his work. His product itself meant little. A celebration was in order, they would hear nothing of his refusing a first-rate seafood meal. They drank, they talked and ate. Invited him back for a weekend of salmon fishing. The food tasted off, a day too old. His napkin, linen, freshly ironed, looked as if the washwater had been lukewarm. He hated cloth napkins but if they had to be used— So the renewed anger: degrees of elegance! Give it up, finally. But he held onto his façade the proper smiles, and wouldn't relax. They needed him to enjoy their generosity, his success. He had to look the part. He convinced them too well, as if he were their intimate. Come, they said, there's the whole afternoon before your ferry. The new athletic club, a steambath and a swim, just the ticket.

The drinks, the excess, convinced him not to drive off in this state: defences and reflexes were down. Plenty of time, they insisted. He sweated and loosened. Their club had a superior gym, no question. Far better than his. But who needed all this? He went regularly, four days a week, a decade of practice. He did weights, swam rigorously. Here the water in the pool felt warm, silken. It embraced him as he couldn't remember being held, not in a long time. The pleasure of sinking to the bottom arrived suddenly, unprepared for. No, no more seductive than a hug from a child.

He left. The fog waited. He had forgotten. The road was slippery, visibility poor. At the terminal the berth was bare, the ferry gone only minutes, already sucked, invisible, into the grey.

He cursed the boat to begin with, then his own lack of discipline. The next ferry left in seven hours. He sat for more than ten irritated minutes in the waiting room, calming himself. It came to him finally: he wouldn't want the circumstance otherwise. A chance, perhaps fated, to explore the dramatic outports, the soul of Newfoundland, its hidden fame.

He drove the Olds as the road led, a kilometre, two, twenty. A steep hill, low trees on either side dripping with the fog's breath. Between the trees, beyond them, the mist faded bushes and rock into a distant chill; soft shapes. All pretty, in its way. Could he live in such a land?

At the crest, closer to the sky, the light was whiter. Such sun as still hovered reflected the particles of fog. The brightness lasted less than half a minute. The road dipped again and new mist encircled the car.

For months, nearly two years, vice-presidencies had ceased to quicken his blood, new company projects held no meaning. What gave him pleasure? His family was gone now, his few friends living only the old patterns. Fishing still excited him, standing by the water, floating on it, the unexpected under the surface, its potential. He could so easily have brought his rod along, the new graphite one. But who would have assumed today's detour, this indirection. Perhaps if he opened the trunk would he find a spinning rod and flashing silver lures? The sea was full of mackerel and cod, the rivers of salmon.

At the bottom of the hill lay a small village, a harbour. A score of houses held onto the land as it slanted down to water. Three narrow piers, eight fishing boats, dozens of lobster traps, green nets drying: a charming moment, below the fog. These little boats would go out to sea through immense waves, could be caught in devastating blizzards. This was not his kind of fishing. Might it once have been?

A small diner, the village's only point of contact with the passing public; its inside door open, an outer screen to protect the opening; two spinning rods, reels in place, line and wire leader threaded and brought back, held tight by hooks from shiny three-inch jigs, leaned beside the door. He went in. A single light by the counter, no one visible. He called. In the corner under a table, sharp movement. He turned. A cat, watching, motionless now. No one came. Well he hadn't wanted anything to eat. He approached the cat. It stood its ground, then made a choice, turned, faded in the shadows. He stepped back into the fog, headed for the car. Felt the draw. The rods. As if calling him, gentle. He walked slowly over, touched the open one, a Jupiter. A Mitchell reel. He picked it up at the ferrule, reached down, held it by the handle. It had nice balance, a light heft. He took it as if it were his own, put it in the car, got in, drove off.

Years and years. He had come up from Philadelphia in the early sixties, feeling Montreal as the edge of the only civilization he knew, the city where Boston, London, Europe stopped. For the while this was enough, a compromise of a life, earning his salary and comforts just as always, yet hovering near the outside, at the rim. To raise the kids, to have outlived his wife— But even then he knew: forever a part of the centre, tied to it with long lines, the ever-renewed U.S. passport, his son's—

The road ahead sloped upwards, the distances loomed an equal grey. Curves, left and right, left again and there a kind of fork. The lesser road headed straight and he took it. In half a kilometre it swung toward the water. He let it guide him; turning back was no alternative. Now there were fields on both sides, fences. He slowed. Ahead a dirt road, little more than a tractor path, led to the right. A sign claimed it as Private Property, instructed him to Keep Out. He angled the ninety degrees and bumped along slowly, gentle enough, a couple of hundred yards. The track made an arc, stopped in a turning circle. He got out. Here was the edge of the sea, a bay really, an inlet he couldn't tell the shape or size of in the fog. A jetty reached into the water, he couldn't see its end. As far as he could go.

Three years back he'd gone beyond Montreal, out to the wilds of the Maritimes, a job with a small company on Nova Scotia's southeast coast, the world suddenly all Pentecostal churches and an undisciplined sea. A perfectly good position, they were delighted, such sophisticated talents. They gave him his time, enough so he could see himself clearly, explain himself with precision and new kindness, feel himself surrounded by empty imitations of the handsome little towns north of Philadelphia he had long ago fled.

He took the fishing rod along. He had only borrowed it. He would return it on the way back. He could have sworn it was his own, it felt so right. He walked out on the jetty. The tide was down, no tracks of sea birds on the mud flat. Would the water beyond be deep enough for anything of size, anything taking a bait as big as this jig? In the fog the world was silent, the water soft as a kitten. The jetty was a rambling thing of lateral boards, some rotted, no evidence of recent use. He stepped carefully over a missing plank, testing with each advance the wood under his feet. How far away was the open ocean? He stood and listened for surf. Nothing. He walked further. Shore had disappeared into the fog. The jetty came to an end. Was it deep enough here— He heard a small splash. He stopped moving, breathing. He stared. Nothing. Suddenly two-three-four splashes. There, on top of the water, mackerel, tinkers, swirling. It would be a school, large. He watched, content at his discovery. The swirl again, and then a new sound, the delicate grind of a reel drag. Someone, fishing out in the fog. From a boat, casting into the school. Again the drag, again the swirl, the mackerel was fighting; a sharp mid-size fish on light line would cause that whir. His mouth had formed a congratulatory, Looks pretty good! but he caught himself. Wasn't he trespassing? With a rod not his own. He sat on the planking.

There, the slow drift of a dory, just at the edge of the thicker fog. A hint of current that far out. The man raised his rod as he brought the fish to the boat. He knelt toward the water. Down where light was strongest his face became clear. The man from the ferry. No anger or sorrow here. Composure.

The dory floated closer. The man cast again, worked his jig, reeled in, nothing. Once more. This time a strike, he set the hook, the mackerel was on. A smaller one this time, barely a minute to bring it in. Again he leaned, grabbed the leader, swung the fish aboard. Did he know he was being watched? By the tinker perhaps? Not the four dead ones in the sack by his feet. The dory slid silently up to the jetty, leaned against its farthermost supports, rested there. The man raised his rod to cast. The line hummed from the old Mitchell and the jig hit the water with a sweet sucking sound. He reeled, working the lure through the stillness. The lure stopped, the rod arced, a mackerel slanted toward the fog. The slim spun graphite turned the tinker gently, headed it to the boat, forty seconds later lifted it on. He smiled. Six was enough.

With an oar he pushed away from the jetty. He rowed in silence to his island. Only recently his. No one would come.

He pulled the dory up the sand. The little beach was his too, he had claimed it. Not so much as a shack on the island, not even a lean-to. He would build one in the next days. Enough wood, certainly. Trees for a small cabin. Deadfall to burn all winter.

He wouldn't need the credit cards. He had savings, plenty, to draw against; the accounts would stay open. With cash he could buy what he needed. He compromised. Foodstuffs in large amounts, hard to secrete, those he purchased. The rest he decided to take. At first he called this, borrow. But he would never return the axe, nor the rods. No one had used the dory all summer; till now. The axe was one of two dozen at the hardware store. Permanent loan. The wealth of the nation, of the previous owner, could allow this in small quantities. In recompense. To settle his mind, he sent cheques, a final public act after leaving the ferry, to four charities. There was a twinge of loss for Misty, the runt, but she was well taken care of. He felt little for his employers. Did they deserve better? Never showing for the meeting in St. Johns, simply opting out, this gave him a boy's satisfaction, small but clean.

One day, if he had to explain, he would invent a story, tell it as quietly as he could. There'd be a man, somewhat like himself. He'd give him a car, an Oldsmobile, and put him on the ferry. There would be fog.

SEEKING THE BOTTOM, AGAIN

PER BRASK

Swimming had always been a really great way to relax for her. Particularly the breast stroke. Where the crawl provided for a lot of activity and exercise in the water it was never conducive to thinking. For that, the quiet gliding movement of the breast stroke was necessary. Swimming under water produced almost superreal experiences, activating, she believed, cetacean memories. A perfect place to strive for meaning. The sensation of the lake's August warm liquid surrounding her body with equal pressure everywhere, filling her ears to reduce sound and altering her vision, brought images to her mind which were vague and fuzzy but nonetheless very homey, safe.

She emerged from the deep. The water in Falcon Lake still tasted the same as it had twelve years ago when she first swam in it, the evidence of acid rain so far only immediately detectable, on the growing brown areas in the crowns of trees and on the sides of fir. A destructive levelling process was insinuating itself into a natural cycle of life and death.

Behind the green foliage, the large scenic windows and the brown roof of the cottage perched on the steep hill could just be made out. The long staircase down to the dock and the small patch of beach, on the other hand, made no attempt at hiding its sixty-six brown steps. Her two kids on the beach digging a huge hole, had decided to settle their ongoing feud long enough to pose a real threat to the lives of several minnows. Her husband was sitting where he'd sat all morning working on a paper he was to deliver in Sweden next week. Her youngest, her eight-year-old son, waved out to her. She waved back, then she dove into the deep again and outwards to where she could no longer see the bottom of the lake. The sudden disappearance of the sandy bottom and the revelation of the darkness of the deep was always a thrill. She felt pulled towards that dark, seemingly bottomless unknown, drawn down to where sight and sound were minimized to the point where she was only aware of her own being, announced by the pressure of the water. She had to come up for more air.

She had come closer to the little island in the middle of the lake than she had imagined and when she turned around towards the shore she was momentarily startled by the smallness of her family. She swatted a horsefly on her forehead and noticed her shrivelled hand. She must have been in the water for quite a long time. Should she swim back in and resume her responsibilities? Her ten-year-old daughter was waving both her arms and jumping up and down, appearing alternately as an "I" and as an "X." Satisfied that she had caught her mother's attention she made big pointing movements with her right hand to her left wrist. Children seemed to have an internal clock telling them meal times. Treading the water a little more actively, the annoyed mother looked towards the preoccupied father on the dock. She felt silly, but finally she made pointing gestures towards her husband trying to tell her daughter that she should ask her father to prepare lunch. The daughter looked briefly towards her father then back to her mother to whom she sent a gesture clearly saying, "Forget it, it isn't even worth trying." The mother smiled to herself and dove back into the deep.

Since her younger brother had told her six months ago that he had been diagnosed with AIDS after a terrible and prolonged bout of pneumonia, Lilly had felt paralyzed. She had turned down all offers of acting jobs and she had been unable to finish the suite of poems which were to complete her second collection, the deadline having now been extended three times and the publication date moved back a year. He had come to Winnipeg from Vancouver to take part in the celebrations of an ACTRA award she'd received in Toronto the previous week but which she had wanted to celebrate in Winnipeg so that her kids and closest friends could participate. At three thirty in the morning after the guests had left and her husband, Mike, had gone to bed after promising to clean up tomorrow, she and her brother sat in the kitchen sharing the last beer and the last cigarette to be found anywhere in the house.

"I'm moving back to the States," Ian began.

"Expanding the business?" Ian's small alternative architectural firm had grown in attractiveness on the market as postmodernism was gaining acceptability in establishment circles.

"No, I'm actually thinking of closing down."

"You are? Why? I thought things were going really well. Besides I didn't think you liked the States very much." Of the two of them, only Lilly had changed her citizenship to Canadian as soon as she could. They had come up here together after she had finished her training at Yale. He had wanted to study architecture in Vancouver, away from any possibility of ever being drafted and she had felt, correctly, that there might be more acting work available to her in Canada, work which actually paid some money, however little. The idea of fighting through the system in New York had seemed thoroughly unattractive to her. In one sense, she could have gone anywhere, but ended up in Canada by an accident of ease whereas Ian had wanted to go because he felt drawn to the architectural and planning challenges provided by the impossible climate. During the '60s the strangest things could make people alter the course of their lives. Still, it was she who had become a Canadian. Ian was still an American.

"I'm going to die. I want to return to . . ."

"Well, we're all going to die at some point, but that doesn't mean . . ." she laughed.

He didn't. "Lilly, I'm not just going to die. I am at this very moment dying."

"Stop that." She paused. "What do you mean you are at this very moment dying? Isn't that a little melodramatic?"

"Well, you'd know that better than I. I've got AIDS and I'm moving to San Francisco." His face looked relieved. Nothing more was exchanged between them for several moments. Lilly had felt completely unable to respond. Faced with the impossible, her mind shut down. She had never actually encountered the possibility of death in her family. Her grandparents were all dead before she was born or had died before she had been old enough to know any different. Her parents were still only in their mid-sixties but, yes, somewhere down along the line in ten, twenty years, perhaps more . . . But her thirty-five-year-old brother? No!

"Why San Francisco?" she finally asked without knowing why.

"I don't want to be a freak in Canada. I want to be part of a community." He'd said it almost as if he were articulating a manifesto. Lilly just sat there. "Look, I'm really sorry to tell you this now. Ruin your celebration. But I thought since we were sitting here alone . . . Well, I just felt that this was the best time. If ever there is a best time." He smiled and began to cry. "I'm sorry. I'm so sorry. I'm so . . . scared." The words were whimpered out through the spittle in his mouth.

"A community of suffering?" She had whispered without expecting an answer as she went to cradle her little brother's head in her bosom.

After the required waiting period of an hour and a half to digest lunch, Lilly was back in the lake, now farther out, closer to the little island. Mike took the kids to go horseback riding at the stables by the townsite. It was understood that, because of her fear of horses, she would not join them. The water was slightly warmer now, though as she moved forward through the water she occasionally glided across cooler patches.

Lunch was good. Mike was a good cook, but his skill at salads in particular had always delighted her. The kids had rushed through it as usual and run off to visit with some distant cousins a few cottages away. During the clean-up Mike had approached her quietly, his calm presence claiming her attention.

"You seem to be withdrawing again . . ."

"No, I'm fine."

"Is there anything you'd like me to do? Or anything you'd like to do? I mean we could talk this through, you know."

"No, I'm just trying to get a hold on things. I'll be fine. Don't worry."

"I'm not worried. But this is the third time you've withdrawn like this in two weeks. We'll only be here another week. We could try to enjoy ourselves a little."

"Well, I'm really sorry that I'm ruining your vacation." She yelled it louder than she'd intended. She knew he'd think of it as a dramatic technique but she really did not have a real grasp of, or connection with, her emotions. Sometimes statements would come out too firmly, sometimes not firm enough. He kissed her on the forehead.

"Okay, I'll take all the kids down to the stables. You can have the afternoon to yourself."

She dove into the deep using all her strength to work against the water. She pulled herself down trying to reach the bottom. Maybe down there she could hold on to something and stay down. She wanted to bring herself to the very brink of death to see if a revelation, a meaning would come clear as she broke through what she imagined to be a barrier, a barrier at once psychological and metaphysical. There had to be some way of knowing. But she could not. The water and her need for air forced her back towards the surface. She felt dizzy and a humming and banging noise filled her mind. It got louder as her head emerged from the water. Then it turned into a roaring whoosh as a motorboat passed inches from her face. In a startled shock she looked towards the disappearing boat as she seemed to see a small person laughing at her with a large, ugly grin. She soon realized that she was looking at a drawing on the boat and that no one on board had taken notice of her.

When Ian had come to visit her in Winnipeg at the beginning of the summer he had looked a little slimmer, his skin had little blotches here and there which looked like eczema. And he looked very tired with big bags under his eyes. When she'd picked him up at the airport he had kissed her and whispered, "I know this isn't going to be an easy visit for you but casual contact is fine and a little kiss on the cheek is not going to kill you." She was going to protest that she hadn't even thought of it, which was true, but his statement had nonetheless removed a nagging, repressed worry.

"We're going to make you all ready to have an AIDS patient around," Ian said in the car as he pulled out rubber gloves and thick paper napkins which he placed in the glove compartment. "Some of these and of these, in case you drive silly and we have an accident. We'll also place them around your house in case I cut myself, that sort of thing."

Lilly was going to interject but with a little sigh she let him go on.

"And I promise not to touch the kids. And when I've left, you all should get tested. Not because anything will have happened but because then you won't have to fret about anything subconsciously. I know that you're just about to object now, but let's do it my way, okay, and everything will be fine."

She was indeed going to object, yell at him, but there was no point. He was right. But worse, the intimacy which had always been theirs had been broken forever. Part of their relationship was already dead.

The sun was beating down. This was the hottest day in memory, but she was lying on the dock just covered by a towel. Suddenly she heard Mike's voice.

"Didn't you hear me calling?"

"No, didn't even hear you come down the stairs. I must have dozed off a little."

"Well come on upstairs then, you'll get a sunstroke this way. Anyway, Fred just called. He wants you to be in Bruce's new play which is to open in Edmonton in November."

"No, I can't."

"Yes, you can. You call him right back and tell him yes."

"But . . ."

"No buts. Call him."

"But what if something should happen to Ian? I'd have to leave rehearsal or I'd have to leave in the middle of the show. I couldn't do that to people I work with."

Mike took a deep disapproving breath. Then he sat down next to her and said calmly, "Listen, I don't want to force you to do anything but I think you should get back into rehearsing a project and you should get back to your book. In fact, I think you should write about what you're going through with Ian's illness."

"I couldn't do that." She was indignant.

"Why not?"

"It would be inappropriate. A betrayal of Ian. Besides what he's going through is one hell of a lot more . . ." She couldn't find the word matching her sense of priority. "Pertinent," she finally added, dissatisfied. "I'd feel like a leech profiteering on his misfortune." She paused and finally she broke out in the crying wail which for the umpteenth time in the past six months had taken a full day to find its release. "It's so unfair. He's so young. He's so good . . ."

Mike put an arm around her. "I know, I know . . ."

"Why?" she asked. "Why?"

There was no answer to be had. Anywhere.

VII

WHERE FAIRY GODMOTHERS COME FROM

GEORGE SZANTO

TENDING THE GARDEN

PER BRASK

WHERE FAIRY GODMOTHERS COME FROM

GEORGE SZANTO

Where Fairy Godmothers come from is not the issue here. For the first thirty-four years of Linda's life, hers never showed; until now she'd not been needed. Still, a personal Fairy Godmother sitting down beside her on the 9:02 shouldn't take Linda by surprise: every day she rubs shoulders with people who make things happen.

The FG, one of those women of indeterminate age, a mature thirty-nine or face-lifted fifty-seven, surely a character actress with great range had she chosen the theater as her profession, wore a brown wool coat, open, and a pink sweater covering a matron's bosom. The coat, cut according to fashion rules half a dozen seasons old, just escaped judgement from twenty-nine fellow travellers. Fifteen glances had fallen on her over-stuffed carpetbag, a relic so antique, so idiosyncratic, could it be chic? But two minutes out of Edgenarrow, once more preparing to bring greatness to their commerce, fifty-eight eyes were lost in the *Journal*, the *Post*, the *Times* and two hundred ninety fingers smudged the newsprint.

A thirtieth head turned to its neighbour person. "How do you do, my dear. I'm Mrs. Boucket."

Linda, musing about an apartment in the city to avoid this daily commute, looked for the first time at the woman beside her. "I'm sorry. Do I know you?"

"Oh no. That is, not precisely. But you did summon me."

"I'm sure I didn't."

"Oh yes, dear. On several occasions. The last time, let me see—" With some difficulty she unzipped the top of her bag: clothing, files, a couple of paperbacks. She pulled out a small notebook, leafed through. "Three weeks ago Tuesday."

Very softly Linda laughed. "Faster than the plumber."

"I'm sorry?"

"Nothing, never mind. Look, you must have me confused with someone else."

"Oh no, I don't think so. You are Linda B—, aren't you?"

"Yes, but I don't think I—" Linda stopped. Twenty or so eyes had turned from their papers. A rare thing, conversation on the 9:02.

"Well, Linda, there we are then." Mrs. Boucket replaced the notebook, struggled to draw the zipper closed—. "Do you mind holding the sides together while I do this?"

Linda, wearing a straight skirt and tight jacket, would have preferred not to. But the women's struggle called for help. Linda bent, felt the blouse at her waist pull loose, squeezed; together they succeeded. Pulling back to her seat she brushed a leg against the corner of her attaché case and felt the nylon of her stocking snag. Damn; yes, on the right calf, a little hole. And a meeting at ten, no time to buy new ones. She felt dishevelled, now would have to rush, a foggy humid day— She scowled, fingered the little tear to make sure Mrs. Boucket saw, then sat back and picked up the newspaper.

"I'm sorry, my dear. But I think I can make it up to you. Now, am I right, you don't remember bidding me to help you?"

Linda took charge. "Mrs. Boucket, please. I have a long day before me and I'd like to read my—"

"Yes yes dear, in just a minute if you want. But I have my job too. Now then. I'll tell you who I am. I'm your Fairy Godmother, here to offer you a contract."

"Mrs. Boucket—"

"I know, it's hard to believe. But truly, you have been asking for me. I've been quite busy, these terrible last days with the Market you know, people are in a truly awful state. Well, we have to set our priorities, just too much work, and my heart isn't what it used to be." She sighed, shook her head.

Linda concentrated on the chess problem. She didn't play.

"At any rate here I am, and you have three wishes. Anything you want, my dear."

Linda ignored her.

"You'll have to tell me before we reach the city. Thereafter the offer becomes void."

Linda stared at her horoscope: Romance takes on significant overtones. Beware of strangers. Don't let small annoyances aggravate you.

"And this offer won't be repeated, Linda. Three wishes, my dear."

Linda, by necessity unaware of the enchanting possibilities the future might bring, shook her head, turned to Mrs. Boucket who held, how curious, a pen; prepared to take notes, but no paper? She squeezed her eyes shut. "I wish you'd go—" Linda's eyes blinked open.

"—away."

And Mrs. Boucket was gone.

Linda glanced across the aisle. A man by the window reading, the seat beside him empty. She stood, reached, a self-conscious movement, for the back of Mrs. Boucket's seat; no one hidden here. She looked up and down the aisle, glanced at seats nearby. No lady of indeterminate age, no overfilled carpetbag.

The train slowed, stopped; Witherton. Linda sat, glanced at the paper, closed her eyes. The chess column must have put her to sleep; a strange dream. Her calf itched, she bent to scratch it and rubbed the hole in the stocking.

A man plumped down beside her. "Hello Linda."

Yes a bad start to a morning. "Hello Harry." Because a couple of years ago they had spent three months as a couple; could she live with him, marry? Both of them were looking, Linda since a year after Ted's accident, a year into widowhood; would she ever find a good man again? With Harry she foresaw the sacrifices, the indulgences: he smoked three packs a day, drank half a gallon of whiskey a week, had tendencies to friendly violence. Take all this in a marriage package? She'd asked him to change these ways of his; he accused her of bossiness, pride. But Linda knew her mind. He rejected her.

Now he grinned. "How've you been?"

She smelled the breakfast whiskey. "Harry, please sit somewhere else."

"That's not very kind. You're looking nice." He touched her sleeve.

"Please Harry!"

Over his glasses the man across the aisle stared.

"No need to shout, Lindy, look you're getting all flushed." He reached to touch her cheek.

She slapped his hand away.

"Ow!"

She turned from him, stared out the window, at the fog they rumbled through. She felt tired. Her head leaned against the cool window glass. How I wish someone simple like that Mrs. Boucket were here instead of this—

Had she said or thought this?

For beside her, smiling, sat Mrs. Boucket, the large bag at her feet.

Harry, on his butt in the aisle, grabbed an armrest, yanked himself up, glared at Linda, sat beside the man across the way, shrugged with irritation, "Don't ask me."

Linda stared at Mrs. Boucket. "Incredible."

"No no, completely normal. A shame, though. You've wasted two of your wishes. And I'm afraid you can't use the last one to wish for three more, that's been tried you see and we've had a ruling. Sorry, not allowed."

Linda whispered, "You're telling me I can have any wish I want?"

Mrs. Boucket nodded, smiled and breathed back, "Of course. That's why you summoned me, isn't it?"

"But I didn't—"

"Now don't make me open my bag again, the requisition's there somewhere but you saw how hard this thing is to zip up. If I recall, you were thinking about sending in the application to work with motor-impaired adults, returning to the skills you'd been trained for during the idealistic sixties, is that right?"

How did she know this? Linda had written for the application, filled it out, then held off; she'd give the company another chance. "You said, three weeks ago—?"

"That's right. After your embarrassment with Mr. Stickler."

Linda, feeling her nape grow warm, hunched her shoulders. Who was this woman? Dan Stickler had asked her to dinner, said he wanted to talk about the Stamen account, she'd hoped otherwise, misunderstood— "But you said I've called you before?"

"Not by name, dear, no, nor even by my function. No no, a woman of your position and respectability wouldn't sit up in bed in the middle of the night and call out, 'Fairy Godmother, Fairy Godmother, I need you.' " Mrs. B. chuckled. "Those days are past. However—" A gentle smile.

Was this to be believed? Come on, Linda, at least humour her, it'll be a great lunch story. "This is ridiculous, Mrs. Boucket—"

"Now think carefully. Before we leave the train, three wishes—oh dear I mean one, I'm really sorry. And you're someone who could use three wishes so well. Some of the others I've been assigned to, it's disgraceful the Organization heeding their calls. Ah well, ours not to reason why. A shame. If it were mine to do, I'd give you the two extra. But of course I can't break up a three-pack."

Linda giggled. "Wishes come in three-packs?"

"Of course. Everything does, good luck *and* bad luck, right?"

"What can I wish for, what kind of thing?"

"I'm sorry dear, I can't guide you through the categories. Though I should warn you, don't be too greedy, even the Organization won't give away a million dollars, and we can't bring back Clark Gable, and you mustn't wish for some nasty person's car to go over a cliff, no not that sort of thing at all. We're a beneficent organization, that's our charter."

Beneficent—! "Can I think for a few minutes?"

"I believe my watch is correct and the train's on time. You have twelve."

If one could make three wishes— The games of girlhood; and yes, more recent times as well. Okay then: a man who loved her for herself and she could love unchanged. Not a lot of money but enough for independence so she wouldn't pass her last years impecunious. Good health while she lived and a quick painless end. The first woman to be come president of the company. Wisdom to advise others in their worldly affairs. Lots of good things. But—truly not possible.

"You have eight minutes, my dear."

"It's hard, one choice."

"Yes, I've been thinking about that too. Now look. I believe I could tell the Organization it was my fault you wasted the first two. I made you tear your stocking, you became angry and wouldn't believe me. Dear dear dear I do wish now I'd never asked your help with my bag, then I wouldn't be in this little mess, but— Yes, my dear, I think I could say that. Except we still have the extra wish to dispose of. And I can't let you have four, that would be unheard of."

"I understand." Ridiculouser and ridiculouser.

"Unless of course," and Mrs. Boucket, conspiratorial, leaned toward Linda, "the fourth proved to be an extremely insignificant wish. Such as," her eyes twinkled in ultra-FG fashion, "you wished your stocking didn't have a hole in it?"

Linda, shaking her head, chortled in disbelief. One wish, three wishes. To wish away a torn stocking— "You think that'd do it?"

"It might. Yes it might. And I'd feel much less badly." She looked at Linda's ready face and bobbed her head.

Linda again felt an itch on her calf, didn't touch it— "Okay. I wish my stocking didn't have a hole in it." She felt nothing. She looked down. One torn stocking. Of course. Come on, Linda, take charge.

Mrs. Boucket, nodding her chin against her bosom, reached a package over. "Here you are, my dear. These are yours."

Linda took the package; stockings, naturally.

"Now then my dear, three minutes."

Too quick. The whole thing was madness anyway, Linda knew this with total clarity. But on the crazy chance— She wished for love. Then the health one. And—between money and career—?

The train slowed, the platform already outside the window—

A successful career, the first woman president, and so on! (Surely money and security would come from her position with the company.)

The train stopped. Linda expected, with a tiny part of her mind, to see Mrs. Boucket and her bag disappear before her eyes. But no, the two women walked off together. Because it seemed the FG needed to dispense some advice or direction, but found the station too noisy, too rushed; or she didn't like the smell. So Linda helped her climb the stairs; her heart, you see—

The fog had not lifted precisely, more a sense it'd never taken charge here, never had the courage to invade the city, the flat building façades had bounced it back to the river, the ocean; wherever. Still, the world remained grey.

At this point Linda usually took a cab. Today they walked. "Well my dear, soon you shall meet your young man, he'll be handsome, and kind, and you'll have great happiness, everything passionate, very romantic. The first night you spend together, he'll give you the night of the tiger, truly gripping. You won't have known such a thing, no, not even with your Ted."

"I beg your pardon? The night of the tiger?"

"That's right, dear. A grappling experience. Now you do understand it'll take a while till you become president of your company, the Organization cannot move against nature, but soon, quick, you'll see the advances. Hard work, yet healthy work, that too, no deviations from your goal. There, aren't you glad we have a contract? And now my dear I have to go, a lady from down south is taking a flight, I must be beside her. Where do I get the airport bus?"

Linda glanced around. "Let's find you a cab, it's the best way there—"

"And I'll check back with you, of course, in— "

"Good, there's one. Hey!" She flagged down the taxi, turned.

But Mrs. B. had disappeared. No one. Not even a carpetbag. How—

"Hey lady you practising your wave?"

She dismissed the cab with the back of her hand, he signalled rudely, she whirled about—and collided with a passing man, stumbled—

He caught her. "Oh I'm very sorry, are you all right?"

"Yes. It's okay." She brushed her skirt straight. "Fine." He was staring.

"Isn't your name—Linda? Linda, ah, Linda— I'm sorry, I've forgotten your last name."

"Yes but— Do I know you?" A day for those words. She hadn't used them on Harry, she should have.

Manny F—. He and she had each presented position papers, the same panel, a conference in T—, four years ago. He'd been impressed by her contribution. They'd all had a drink after, the whole panel. She'd been called away, her husband in an accident wasn't that it? He hoped everything had turned out all right.

"No, he was killed."

"Oh I'm terribly sorry."

"It seems like a long time ago, Mr. F—."

"It must have been very difficult."

So they exchanged clichés, waiting for the other— But why, in truth? They both had appointments in less than half an hour, they each—

Yes she would be free for lunch, though not till one-thirty; she took charge of the moment, reorganizing her agenda on the spot; easy enough to opt out of her regular Friday luncheon, three women friends, executives in their companies, always at 2:00 p.m., a couple of drinks, sharing professional difficulties, the few triumphs.

So Manny and Linda met, ate soup and quiche, talked, found they had much in common. He'd just transferred to the city, still living at a hotel, looking for a place, the new job offered great possibilities. She too needed an apartment, had been in Edgenarrow for nine years, the job demanded so much time, she ought to be in town, yes she'd looked though half-hearted, oh for over a year, couldn't make a decision, it depended on if she kept her job, fine work and an excellent company but— Yes he knew what she meant, was offered his job a year ago but got himself near the point of committing himself to public service, give his talents to the Save the Children Fund or Amnesty International or some such thing, they paid by and large nothing but— Yes he believed in the greatness of his corporation, still he couldn't get himself to decide, ever since his wife died—

Now Linda offered condolences. An accident also, at the lake in Minnesota, drunk teenagers in a motorboat swamped the canoe Nancy, dear sweet Nan, had been paddling, Nan must have hit her head; terrible. But the coincidence! because Ted, her poor Ted, had broken his neck diving from the ten-metre board at the Edgenarrow Country Club pool, new, olympic-size. Death by water, twice. It linked them in tragedy as well.

When they looked up it was quarter to four, the waiters patiently polite. "Will you have dinner with me?" She could have said this, was liberated enough; or he.

"Yes."

They would meet, after he dealt with a client and she finished a report. Would this be the night of the tiger?

Her report proved too complicated, Monday she'd be in by eight. Manny was her kind of man: tall and solid, a careful smile sometimes crossing his lips, light blue eyes under salt-and-pepper eyebrows demanding attention; had James Dean lived to thirty-eight— So she saw him.

And he her? Later he told her, honesty foremost: a Marilyn. The one and only. Better because, as he'd always seen it in the movies, Marilyn's body was too skinny. Now Linda, her fine blonde hair, rich red mouth, the warm curves, the sway of her walk, her voice both strong and soft: what more could he desire? So he gave his client excellent terms, the man left happy and quickly.

Linda and Manny dined, laughed, looked into each other's eyes. They felt the weight of the evening; a splendid burden. She heard the delicacy of his phrasing as he asked, would she spend the night with him? He recognized the pleasure in her response: if he'd not asked she would have requested. They left the restaurant arms about each other and in love.

His hotel room, respectable, lived-in, stocked with fine spirits: they sipped cognac and held hands, kissed, they had the whole night, perhaps all weekend; perhaps—

They undressed each other. Her short Marilyn weighed in at a hundred-sixty, staggering bosom and chubby hips. He, suitless, bellied out and shouldered down.

They lay in the bed, embraced, slow, testing, learning. Yes they'd seen each other clearly enough, she the juicy large-bottom perfection he'd searched for, he the rangy fearless reward for waiting. Not blindness, but love. The passion built, built, built— and the night of the tiger began.

Daylight filled the room. They'd slept little, now lay awake holding each other. She wondered, would this have happened without Mrs. Boucket? Might she have bumped into Manny anywhere? Suddenly she felt uncertain of Mrs. Boucket's actual existence, had it really been—? Wasn't she just a notion, a metaphor for their accidental meeting? Linda, working late the last two weeks, sleeping badly, getting on the train exhausted: surely she'd slept her way to the city. Mrs. Boucket, what a delightful invention!

Manny, kissing Linda, breathed, "Do you believe in Fairy Godmothers?"

She shuddered in his arms. "Why do you ask that?"

"Well it was the strangest thing. Yesterday morning, at breakfast,

I go to the Greek around the corner, we'll try it later if you want. The place was crowded, usually is, I was eating my eggs and a woman asked could she share my booth. I looked at her, tough looking lady, wore a dark sort of suit, not exactly what you want to look at over breakfast but I was nearly done anyway so I said sure. And she said, 'My name is Cupious, I'm relieved to find you at last.' Well this seemed strange so—"

Linda put a finger to his lips. "So you got irritated with her at first and—"

"No, I figured she'd mixed me up with someone else and I—"

Linda pressed her finger harder. "You talked for a while and she said you'd been sort of calling out to her and—"

"That's right, how'd—"

"And she offered you three wishes."

He swung around, stared down to her face. "How'd you know that, Linda? How?"

He seemed close to angry, or scared. She smiled, shook her head, told him about Mrs. Boucket.

Manny and Ms. Cupious had parted ways not moments before he'd bumped into Linda, "They weren't taking any chances, were they?" They both laughed, only a touch nervous, then made excellent love and referred to it as the morning of the tiger; it sounded wrong but had felt great. At the Greek's she asked him, "And your three wishes?"

"Linda—can we spend the weekend together?"

She took his hand. "As long as you like." She waited. "Don't you want to tell? I'll tell you mine."

"Go ahead."

She did.

They made eminent sense to him.

"And yours?"

"You really want to know?"

She nodded, brisk and eager.

"First, a wife who loves me very much and who'll always care for me."

She squeezed his hand hard.

"Then, three perfect children, two boys and a girl."

Kids? Three?! Ai!

He played with her fingers. "Ms. Cupious thought two would be sufficient."

Bless Ms. Cupious. Linda waited. Smiled.

He turned his eyes away.

"And the last wish?"

"Linda—I don't think I should tell you."

"Well, if you prefer—"

He looked down at his eggs. "I'd rather not."

"Will you one day?"

He nodded. "Probably."

Instant happiness. They married three months later, honeymooned on St. Thomas in the Caribbean far from fog, ice and hail, avoided all motorboats, outrigger canoes, swimming pools and diving boards. Ongoing happiness.

After a year of marriage Linda went to the hospital direct from the office; Robert was born; she returned a week later. For Denise she agreed to take a month off, knew she'd lose time, begrudged it. They bought a penthouse.

The honeymoon ended during their fourth anniversary. She learned of his third wish. Each year on their wedding date, children baby-sat at home, they holidayed, to reinforce the initial moment, on an island: Sardina, Montreal, Manhattan, now Key West; many nights, many tigers. A pretty room overlooking the sea, a fine balcony, Manny ready to blend up the margaritas. But no ice. Manny went to look for ice. Manny didn't return, not after five, eight, ten minutes. Linda went to look for Manny. Yes, the ice machine worked fine, yes the girl believed she'd seen the lady's husband talking with Big Daisy who was cleaning around the corner. Yes there stood Daisy's cart in front of 307. Linda looked. No one. She called quietly, "Manny darling?" No Manny. A light knock on the door of 307. No answer. Never will Linda know why she tried the handle of 307, why 307 wasn't locked. She stepped into the room. On the bed, sticking out from under the gleaming black buttocks of Daisy the hundred-ninety pound chambermaid: Manny, knees to toenails.

Linda fled.

Manny returned in silence. Linda lay in the bed under sheet, blanket, and coverlet. Manny made the margaritas. Linda squeezed the pillow down on her head against the blender's whir. Manny drank two, three, many margaritas.

She hadn't the strength to take charge. "Why?!!"

Tears, recriminations, guilt, dread, rage, lust, shame, fear, pride; yes, and mangled love as well.

Manny's third wish: to become a chartered libertine. Nan, his sweet Nan, such a good person, would never have understood; at times he wanted her dead, he could never have left her, he remained ever faithful. So after her death, his semi-desire fulfilled, such culpability cancered inside him till he felt it ready to burst through his skin; this was when he came close to embracing public service—either that or suicide. A year of agony. Then he met Ms. Cupious. His third wish, a case of modified satyriasis and the courage to act on it, no more than any man his age might ask for, all quite normal. He'd had it now, four-plus years' worth, a woman a day at least. No question, it was a disease. And he loved it.

"I'm not enough for you?" Linda couldn't cry any more.

"My contract with the FG—for me, to be satisfied with one woman, it's impossible."

"Ohhhhhhhh——!!"

Linda shared the agony with her Friday lunch friends. They drank an extra martini; and Cointreau with a second creme caramel. Their discomfort told her everything. Yes, over the years Manny had entered them each; no, not satisfying, not at all. She must see he loved her, only her, the contact of Manny with others was merely physical, he needed their bodies, any woman's body; it didn't matter who lived inside.

Recovery took a while. What did they see in him, those women—a balding stoop-shouldered man with a little pot belly? How could anyone other than herself love him; in any sense? Among Linda's indirect responses, great relief: so wise her decision to wish for health. No wonder Manny kept catching some little thing, at times so weak with flu or the grippe their normal life, from budget to lust, always suffered.

He would never detail to her the other fine large women he'd practised raking. A great range of shapes, chunky or angular, bulbous or muscled, older and newly padded or still clinging to their baby fat. His specialty, widows like and unlike Linda. Some widows, he'd learned, were inconsolable; but many were not.

Through hard work, excellent judgement, taking full charge of dangerous responsibilities and succeeding where others feared to grapple, Linda became president of her company. She and Manny fought: so little time for him and the children. They argued at first about his never-ending randiness, his condition; for he had committed himself, all open now, to these pleasures.

In their separate ways they had become successful people and, when the sums were totalled, felt they could believe this: that they loved each other. Theirs a marriage built like many, their ascendant careers patterned like many; as these were surely meant to be, and their dalliances as well. Yes, Linda also. Finding an inferior man to satisfy a moment proved easier far than finding the perfect husband; anyway him she had. They lived out the patterns of their time and considered themselves lucky.

But they asked, Why? And, How?

Hundreds of times, perhaps a thousand, Linda's mind had re-pictured the 9:02 on that fateful Friday morning. Through the years the image dimmed, became unrealler and unrealler. She found many explanations: at one extreme the character actress, perhaps a professional but more likely a jokester, poking at Linda, mocking her life; at another, the overwrought imagination in her.

Of course they talked about it, one of those couples that tell each other everything, or nearly, and with increasing frequency they argued; this their very special upper mid-life crisis.

Manny's unshakable stance at these times: "But I had an encounter too!"

"I can't believe it. Not in this day and age."

"You're a cynic, my sweetheart."

It grew, it became the largest battle of their lives: was the FG hypothesis necessary? Or could they alone have reached such present happiness?

Linda: The meeting an accident, in their city she could've bumped into any of a hundred men, a thousand, and fallen in love. (She didn't quite believe this; why not? hard to remember.) Manny: Their meeting a construction, the two FGs had all but thrust them into embrace.

Linda: Children and health follow naturally on good nutrition. Manny: So why do I get sick and you bloom? (Linda smirked.)

Linda: My professional success, your sexual success: the result of commitment, devotion and hard work. Manny: And to find the courage to live our convictions?

Linda: You're a romantic. Manny: My great good fortune.

A stand-off. Tense, often bitter, threading its way into every aspect of their lives, threatening to destroy their monument, their marriage, their family, their home.

Counsellors, seen one on one or as a couple, proved useless; how can you convince a shrink your Fairy Godmother started it all?

A single hope: if they existed, bring back the FGs.

How?

Linda's vague memory, that Mrs. Boucket would contact her again. When? Unclear.

Manny's, that Ms. Cupious had said something about a ten-year check-up; or was it twelve? Perhaps seven— No, their tenth anniversary awaited, a few days off.

A foggy night, appropriate, and they went to dinner, their celebration (no islands for six years now): to have lasted a decade, two fine kids, so much strife but yes, somehow, together against the world—

For the last weeks as she'd pull her stockings on a niggle had itched in Linda's mind; then her calf began to tickle; and she, who with agnostic certitude doubted the existence of FGs, remembered a torn stocking, its replacement ready before the wish, but more important the prickle of memory, Mrs. Boucket's words, was there a wish prior to Linda's own? that if Mrs. B. had never asked Linda for help, the stocking wouldn't have torn.

Ridiculous. The vaguest memory of a non-event.

At their happy dinner they argued less, considered more. She described her dubious recollection: a moment in a story that hadn't happened on a commuter train to chance.

Manny said, "Then you're thinking—"

"Yes. Maybe— Might I have one more wish." She shook her head. "If—" But no, no. Impossible. FGs don't exist.

"But the moment. If you remember—?"

"Invented."

That further wish, yes, highly improbable; he conceded this. If ever it had existed, it could no longer be. After all, how many times in ten years does one make a wish, minor, accidental: make tomorrow a sunny day, let our side win, oh to be on time—

Linda knew, but didn't admit: for her, in the years since the train encounter, no casual let alone serious wish had escaped her, neither word nor thought. Such a thing would have seemed, well, sheer sacrilege. Despite her lack of belief. Not even, in their worst days: Manny I wish you wouldn't—

"So. Shall we try?"

"What do we have to lose?"

They held hands, "For us," and toasted in chocolate cake and cognac: "We wish to see our Fairy Godmothers once again."

At the next table a couple in their twenties smiled at the fat romantic old people.

Home well before midnight, the children long asleep. A final B&B. Eleven-twenty, high in their penthouse, holding hands at the window, Manny and Linda saw nothing through the fog, not even the streets below. They kissed. The fog embraced them, brought them their due: the night of the tom-and-momcat. If Marilyn and Jimmy were alive today . . . Quarter to twelve, heightened breathing; the doorbell rang. "Who the hell—" They listened. It rang again. They leapt apart, jumped into pyjamas, grabbed dressing gowns. Again it rang.

Through the fishtank peephole, two women, one holding a valise, the other a heavy bag, the sort of ladies who sell *Watchtower* and *Awake*! Manny threw the door open. "Who are you? How'd you get past the guard?"

The short stubby woman smiled, the tall skinny one scowled. "You people are just impossible to find at home, I mean together. May we come in?"

"But—"

"Don't you recognize us, my dears? Here is Ms. Cupious, and I'm Mrs. Boucket. From the Organization."

"Incredible." Linda stared.

The ladies held their stance.

Manny stared; till— "Oh. Well. Please. Come in. You must."

They entered. They sat in the living room. No, they'd keep their coats, what a chilly night; yes cozy here; still— And Mrs. Boucket's heart, not what it once was.

A smile to Manny, and Linda made the grand, the conceding gesture: "You were right, my darling." And to the ladies: "I'm so glad you heard my wish. Thank you for coming."

The FGs looked at each other. "What wish?"

"Tonight. We wished you here."

The FGs smiled, the one gently, the other grim. "If only it were so. No, a happy coincidence. It's the warranty. We've tried to find you at home together for near to a month now. You're on the list, of course."

"The list?"

"For the ten-year inspection. There's been some trouble, we understand."

"But how do you—"

Ms. Cupious, stern, examined them. "You can hardly visit four counsellors without every computer in town vibrating."

Manny jerked up. "They wouldn't dare— My reputation—"

Mrs. Boucket smiled. "I think Ms. Cupious exaggerates. But at the Organization we *are* equipped for research."

"But how could you—"

Mrs. Boucket leaned to her bag. "I can show you the list."

"No no that's fine." Linda shook her head. "I think I need a drink. What can we offer you ladies?"

A little gracious refusal, some insistence, three decisions. Manny mentioned herbal teas. Oh what kind? Mrs. Boucket should come look, he'd bring ice and glasses for the others.

Linda and Ms. Cupious assessed each other. Linda took charge. "You're right, we've had a hard time in the last months, years even. But my assessment shows—"

"I think we should wait till Mrs. Boucket returns."

"Of course."

Silence.

Linda, trained to probe from silence: "And how many clients does the Organization have?"

"Many. More and more all the time."

"You work in all parts of the country then, with all kinds of people."

"Yes to the first, no to the second."

"I see. And what kind of people?"

"Our mandate limits us, thank goodness, to the upper middle class, with exceptions among the middle class, such exceptions to be documented in careful detail by an FG advisor committed to overseeing the case. We take on only those in stress situations, presently blocked in their work but with the ability, when properly motivated, to succeed."

"Yes." Linda could see tiny print, article four on the memorized Charter. "I agree. Private philanthropy is essential. Once I considered such work myself. Do you have difficulty raising money?"

"My dear, we're a federal agency, supported by your tax dollar."

"No! Not really."

"Have no concern. Independent analysis, both statistical and from the field, has proven that by rescuing excellent people such as yourselves, by saving them from non-productive and/or deviant work, for example your old cripples or Manny's starving foreign brats, the agency pays for itself through increased tax revenue. Productivity is money."

"Impressive."

"Yes."

Silence. That woman, so machinelike: how could Manny ever have accepted her for his FG. Linda felt a growing uneasiness. The drink would help. "And how did you locate me, both of us, in the first place."

"My dear, ninety percent of our budget is devoted to investigation. Our research allocation is the third largest among this country's intelligence agencies. Research precedes stabilization."

"I see." She should ask— Something nagged— She heard a small clatter. "Excuse me."

"Of course."

Another bang, a solid object falling, not breaking. She found Manny in the pantry. Mrs. Boucket sat on a shelf. His pyjama bottoms lay at his ankles, the hem of the FG's dress lay bunched at her waist, her legs had wrapped themselves around Manny's hips, cans jiggled on the shelves. Linda said, "Manny darling not now.

It's rude to keep Ms. Cupious waiting so long."

"Sorry sweetheart, I'm almost done. Why don't you get the ice. We'll be with you in a flash."

Linda did, and they were.

"Mrs. Boucket, on the train, how did you disappear?"

"Why, my pencil of course. It's a tranquilizer-stun. Very handy. And then I walked away. Shall I show you?" She bent again to her bag.

"No please, that's fine. But—you also reappeared?"

Her eyes shone. "We must keep some of our methods secret, don't you think? Or you'd never believe in us." She sat back. "Now then, how can we help?"

"You've already put us aright, Fairy Godmother. How lucky we are. Thank you." Manny and Linda held hands.

TENDING THE GARDEN

PER BRASK

Cuts. By definition, pruning is the removal of plant parts. You remove the parts by making cuts—with your thumbnail or fingers, with shears or saw. The effectiveness of your pruning will be determined by how and where you make these pruning cuts. Using the right tools and using them properly is important to pruning effectively.

David Penner was an excellent amateur gardener. His property, which was enclosed by tall trees and thick bushes, all well pruned and shaped, had often been visited by students of architecture, many of whom he had taught the rules of functional space.

At forty-eight, David was an architect whose environment reflected his professional passions. His home, like his garden, was designed in exceedingly good taste: the several levels of floor space created the illusion of movement and the wallpapers and carpets, judiciously selected for their subtle hues of white, grey and beige, combined to make a simple walk through the Penners' house a peaceful experience. The furniture and even the art hanging on the walls seemed to placate, enhance and compliment their home's dominant colour scheme.

Salix alba "Tristis." Golden weeping willow. Left to its own way, it will head too low to furnish usable shade. Stake up a main stem and keep it staked right up to 15-18 feet. Shorten lower side branches and remove them as they lose their vigour; keep growth directed into a main stem and high-branching scaffold limbs. This treatment will give you a tree you can walk under.

David Penner's yard was, of course, a model of the very best landscaping. It had been sculpted to create a sense of lush well-being. The tall and well-shaped bushes set off against the rock garden's many tiers (Penner disliked lawns) sloped calmly towards the central large swimming pool. In order to integrate this pool, which had been his wife's desire, Penner had designed it in soft, irregular curves around an island planted with birch trees and shrubs. Access to the island was gained via a wooden bridge arching across the pool. The job of cleaning out leaves from the pool had been awarded to the neighbour's teen-aged son for a small weekly sum.

When he walked about in his yard wearing rubber gloves and sporting a pair of pruning shears, Penner was at peace. In this designed environment everything felt natural. He could think while cutting a twig here and shortening a branch there. Some of his best ideas had their birth in this garden; well, actually, over the past ten to twelve years probably all of them. The quiet beautiful enclosure inspired him and he had integrated it into his life and thoughts. This was the place where the pressure, built up in the course of a hectic day, could seep out of his being.

On this particular day, David Penner had more than his share of unpleasantness to deal with and, in the main, through no fault of his own. For example, he'd had to visit a synagogue he had designed in order to check on complaints about water seepage and noisy washrooms. The rabbi had been furious.

"But Rabbi Herschel, I must object to your tone of voice. The seepage in the southeastern corner is due to a construction error, not a design error."

"That's easy for you to say, Mr. Penner."

"Well . . .?"

"What about the noise from the washrooms? It's quite embarrassing when people go downstairs and then a few minutes later . . ."

David Penner had laughed. He smiled now as he recalled the incident. Finally he had convinced the rabbi that he was not to blame for the problems the congregation was finding with the building. But even so, David promised to make certain that the various contractors and subcontractors would attend to correcting their mistakes at the earliest possible moment. He refused to have his name associated with shoddy workmanship.

"Are you otherwise satisfied with the building, Rabbi Herschel?"

"Oh yes, it is a beautiful synagogue . . . Mr. Penner, do you believe?"

"I beg your pardon?"

"Do you?"

"What has that to do with anything?"

"I just wondered . . ."

"This is a fabulous, well-functioning space. What more do you want?"

David had left quite abruptly. The kind of nonsense he had to put up with in the course of creating spaces for clients! The garden provided just the right kind of relief.

> *Suckers*: Any unwanted shoot. If you catch suckers when they are very small and tender, you can snap them off or rub them off. Larger ones should be broken from the plant with a firm, brisk outward and downward snap.

David and Martha had been married for almost twenty-one years. They had met in interlibrary loans where they both worked evenings during their graduate student years. It had not been love at first sight. Their mutual attraction had grown over a period of about a year and a half during which they had learnt to appreciate each other's sense of organization and seriousness of purpose.

Martha, forty-six since yesterday, was still a beautiful, petite woman with black hair and penetrating brown eyes. She was a surgeon of considerable repute and there was some talk of her becoming the chief executive officer of a new hospital, currently in the early planning stages. The move would mean a change to an administrative position for Martha, an area of work in which she felt quite competent and one which she happened to enjoy. There was also "some small possibility" that David Penner might be contracted to design the hospital should it become reality. A sense of anticipation had developed in the Penner household lately over this matter. But its realization depended on a good deal of political will and timing in order to ensure sufficient financing. It was nonetheless a delightful hope to live with.

David and Martha had no children. They had decided early on not to start a family until they had both finished their graduate studies and had established some footing in their chosen careers. A few years after receiving their degrees, they began trying to have children. It had proved a rather lengthy and eventually unfruitful struggle. A great strain was placed on their relationship when they discovered that they would not be able to produce children due to David's low sperm count. After a brief period of some disappointment they realized that they would have to learn to live with this fact. They discussed the possibility of adoption briefly, but neither felt it to be the right solution for them. There was something intriguing about the process of creating and then shaping lives when they had considered the idea of having children of their own, but it seemed incompatible with the idea of adoption.

They had soon forgotten the desire to have children and David had come to feel blessed by his inability to father children. His life would have been quite altered and the pace of his career very different.

David and Martha Penner enjoyed good company and good dinners and the people they preferred to most others were Michael and Elly Ott.

Michael and David had known each other since high school where they had been chief competitors for girls and the captainship of the rowing team. Now, they preferred taking small trips on the river in Michael's little red motorboat during late summer afternoons, followed by a drink (martini for David, bloody Mary for Michael) in the Press Club. (During the winter months they would go straight to the club.) Michael was a political commentator with substantial clout in civic affairs and occasionally their talks at the club would last right through till closing time.

David loved this time with Michael; in fact, he loved Michael a great deal. He balanced so pleasantly David's own concerns with more practical aspects of life. Perhaps, David often wondered, the two of them simply reflected the age-old attraction of opposites? But David was glad that he had met Michael when they were both so young and that they had maintained their friendship. He was aware that he would not have been able to build a friendship like theirs later in life. And without someone like Michael around, David's life would have missed the sense of symmetry he provided.

A couple of times a month the Otts and the Penners would get together to play bridge. Elly Ott was a wizard at this game and her prescience never ceased to amaze David. He enjoyed these evenings.

Martha and Michael had carried on an affair for many years; at least David had known about it for the past ten or twelve. (He was certain that Elly also knew about it.) And until now it hadn't bothered him.

Malus: Crabapple. Deciduous trees. Require regular annual pruning. Neglected they tend to produce a complicated tangle of branches.

David's architecture firm was not one of the largest around but over the years he had built up a solid reputation for quality work. His clients were usually more than satisfied, which gave David a unique position in a complex market, one which he guarded carefully. He had three other architects, four technicians, and two administrative assistants working for him. The other architects in the firm were usually recent graduates on their way to larger firms or to starting firms of their own. Working for David Penner gave a young graduate an advantage when moving on in his career. David screened, monitored and supervised every account with which his firm became involved. In this way, all who worked for him eventually were exposed to the care and precision he put into every project. Penner & Associates could easily, had David wanted, have moved into a more aggressive position but his ambitions did not drive him towards running a large, unwieldy concern. He had, in fact, in most ways already fulfilled his ambitions— establishing a business and a life over both of which he felt in complete control.

He enjoyed his firm very much, though at times the people working for him proved irritating. He sometimes found it necessary to enter into a "friendly" tussle with some young architect. Many of these architects of the younger generation were much too inclined to involve themselves in political issues and David would voice his disapproval openly, to associates working for him and to students at the local university where he was occasionally invited to give guest lectures. These young people were primarily interested in discussing urban planning, zoning laws, or governmental funding practices whereas solutions to the concrete problems under discussion always demanded attention to line, function and materials. It was an aspect of their growth as architects for which David Penner had little patience, and he would at times get quite insistent and loud during these tussles. If the young professional in question happened to be one of his own associates he had been known to instruct the person to sit down and get back to work. Once he even fired a particularly zealous woman who had only been with the firm for two weeks but who seemed to have talked about nothing but "planning and building for people" from the moment she entered the door till the moment David sent her out again.

She had been the one hiring mistake David had ever made. And this single case had nagged at him since it had taken place. Now, walking in the garden, shears in hand, David Penner could even smile at such memories and feel that perhaps he had overreacted to a young woman who sooner or later would have to wake up to the real world in any case. However, what had been done had been done and she really did represent a type he could not tolerate.

> Chrysanthemums need growth control. Allowed to grow unchecked, they'll be sprawling by blooming time. For sturdy plants and big flowers, pinch them frequently beginning at planting time by removing tips of new plants.

The most devastating moment in David Penner's life had happened the previous evening during the celebration of Martha's forty-sixth birthday.

It had not been a large gathering. Michael and Elly were there, of course, as were Martha's older sister Karla and her lover Peter, one of David's young associates and her husband, three or four doctors from Martha's hospital with their spouses, and a couple of city administrators. A small, but substantial gathering. Everyone there knew one another and enjoyed each other's company. It was, in short, the kind of well-put-together occasion for which Martha was so renowned. Or rather, it would have been had it not been for Martha's sister Karla. David and Martha had briefly entertained the possibility of not inviting Karla and Peter but as members of the family they couldn't very well be left out. David's own family was fortunately geographically far away now, and he had to deal with them only for short periods of time. But Martha's family, especially her sister, was a constant in their lives.

Karla was an actress of limited success and David couldn't help but feel that she was suffering from the most evil form of jealousy of Martha. Her jealousy seemed to increase with the developing fortunes of Martha's career. Karla had, in addition, the very bad habit of drinking too much before dinner every time she and Peter visited "Dr. and Mr. Penner" as she called them. And in spite of warnings to the contrary from both Martha and Peter she had been quite drunk by the time dinner had been served the previous evening. During most of the dinner she had sat very quietly and simply gazed at Martha in what seemed like amazement. Occasionally she'd giggled to herself, but no one had paid much attention to her.

However, during David's speech at the table after dessert, as he elaborated on Martha's outstanding qualities, Karla suddenly called out:

"Don't forget to mention that she's both a wife and a mistress."

"I beg your pardon, Karla?"

"Come on, David, she and Michael have one great hot affair going. I must say I was somewhat surprised, Sis."

"Please Karla . . . I don't think . . ."

Martha tried in vain to make her sister shut up. David had felt paralyzed.

Finally the awful event ended with Karla's departure. As she left she said to Martha: "I didn't want to ruin your birthday. I'm so sorry. I don't know what came over me." The rest of the evening had gone well, despite the occasional pregnant pause when people would actively try to forget Karla's interruptions. Elly had behaved as if all was well and fine.

David, though, had not felt very well since the incident. A fog had enveloped his mind and clouded the world around him. He knew that both Martha and Michael knew that he'd known of their affair for a long time and that he really didn't find it a very important issue. But now as he looked into the pool in the garden he was still furious beyond any anger he had ever known. He found it incredulous that Martha would allow herself to be quite so stupidly, so stupidly . . . indiscreet. Obviously he could no longer trust her to keep her sense of control.

> *Pruning Standard Roses*. Objective in pruning tree roses is to keep crowns symmetrical and branches evenly spaced. If you remove an entire branch, cut it flush to the trunk or stem. Be careful not to remove branches that are essential for a balanced crown.

As dusk was gently settling in the sky and the garden grew quite dark, Martha came out into the yard, tired from her day at the hospital.

"Hello darling, I thought you might be out here. I have another exploratory tonight, but what do you say we go downtown and get something nice and quick, perhaps . . ."

At this moment David grabbed Martha's arm and yanked her down the first couple of tiers forcing her to fall the rest of the way to the pool. As she lay unconscious a few feet from the bridge David dragged her body across it to the island and hidden among the tall trees he pushed her face into the water. With his right foot he held her head down gently for a few minutes. A small flock of birds rose from the other side of the island and flew over them.

Then he turned her around and started to administer mouth-to-mouth resuscitation. Satisfied that the procedure was futile, he went in to call an ambulance. As he was about to dial he noticed the pruning shears still in his hands. It was fortunate, he thought, that he had not, in the heat of the moment, decided to use them on Martha. He took the shears and his rubber gloves to the toolshed. He came back. Put on water for coffee. And with a deep sigh he dialed emergency.

After the ambulance left he carefully packed as much of Martha's clothes as he could force into her seven large matching suitcases. The rest he stuffed into garbage bags. Then he called Goodwill.

Driving to work the next morning appropriately late and only to make a brief appearance, David Penner felt that the dense, dark fog which had settled over his mind had finally lifted and that he was ready again to take clear-headed control of his demanding life.

VIII

LINT-READER

GEORGE SZANTO

LOVE AND GROCERIES

PER BRASK

LINT-READER

GEORGE SZANTO

Per— Enclosed my treatment, brief version, for the screen-play of Stephanie Queen's (is she two people?) LINT-READER. You're quite right—one of those novels I wish I'd written myself.

G.

Summertime. An eight-year-old boy, blue jeans, green shirt. A woman, about thirty-five, fabulously beautiful skin as from an Oil of Olay advertisement, hair dishevelled, walking quickly then running along Boston's Commonwealth Avenue. She stops for a moment, uncertain. Looks back— A deep blue Chevy is following, a hundred fifty feet back. On the woman's face, panic.

"Please Mummy, can't we rest?"

His mother, her lips squeezed tight, holds firmly to his wrist and yanks him forward. Rush hour, sticky August. The streets and sidewalks full, bulky sweaty people pushing to get home. The Chevy, its grill a grinning leer, stares at the woman and boy.

A crowd at the corner, waiting for the light to change. The mother, Angie O'Tee, grabbing the boy at the elbow, jostles other pedestrians as she forces a path open to the curb. Two impatient women curse her. A dozen, a hundred legs block her way. Desperate, she glances around, spots—oh thank goodness!—an empty taxi. But two bankers step onto the street and steal it. The light turns green, the thick crowd surges across the street. Angie glances back. The terrible Chevy bridles at the intersection. Suddenly she realizes: here they'll make their move! She grasps the boy, Leslie, by the shoulder, fear now spread across his face also, when suddenly—can it be? a miracle!—a cab drops a passenger right by her side. Angie throws her arm round Leslie's waist, pries open the cab door, sweeps him inside, lunges in after.

"Where to, lady?"

She turns, squints out the back window. The evil Chevy is two cars behind. Three men in the front seat, four in back. No question—agents of the Council for Security Matters! "Logan

Airport. Our flight's in twenty-five minutes. We make it, you get an extra ten.

The cabbie's accelerating answer thrusts the boy and his mother deep into their seats.

Angie drops her head, cups her brow in her palms, begins to relax.

But a look of anxiety crosses Leslie's face. He leans close to her and whispers: "Mummy, what about money—"

Angie nods, shuddering. In instant decision she closes her eyes, makes two tight fists, directs the entirety of her focus at the cabbie and, with the whole of her mind, she pulls. Very very very hard.

The cabbie, dodging traffic, suddenly turns and grins. "I like you, lady. Know what it said in my horoscope today? A favour to an unknown person brings great changes. I'm going to take you to Logan for free."

Angie's mind pulls yet tighter. How much stretch can be left? "We're going to Burlington Vermont."

"Heck, I'm not doing anything tonight, I'll drive you up. Nice looking kid you got there."

"Thank you." But the immense pull, the fourth in as many days, has left Angie's insides whirling with nausea. She opens the window. Moving air dries the sweat from her face. She dares to look back.

She cannot see the deadly Chevy! They've lost it!!!

CUT TO: A college campus. Spring, 197-. A sanitary laboratory. Two beds. On one, Angie, ten years younger. On the other, Brad O'Tee. Fellow students. They have just met, lying there. They talk. They are getting $156.42 apiece ($200 minus taxes, social security and retirement) for serving as human subjects, guinea pigs to test, supposedly, a new form of aspirin specially made for headaches. The experimenter, Dr. Gorm, short of stature, his face a pallid grey, a man who regularly needs to stop his smile from devolving to a sneer, gives them each an injection. They fall asleep. Instantly they dream: nails drawn from brains, brains limp and shapeless, brains repackaged as in a kind of cellophane, brains reborn. They wake, tell each other their dream: it was the same dream! They reach out from their beds: across to the other, fingers clench. They stand. Their lips meet.

CUT TO: Brad, Angie and their twelve-week-old son Leslie. At the doorway of their home, the parents are going out. Their first movie in months, Brad tells the baby-sitter.

Suddenly Leslie screams. The sitter tries to comfort him. No good. Brad and Angie, grinning sheepishly to the sitter, try to sneak away.

Suddenly Brad's hand jerks to his stomach. "My navel! It's tickling like crazy! Anyway I don't want to be at a movie, I want to stay home with Leslie. What a terrific kid he is."

Angie insists they go. She argues with Brad, starts to leave by herself— Suddenly she scratches the front of her waist, discovers—and says—she wishes for nothing more in the world than to be with dear little Leslie.

Suddenly Leslie giggles.

CUT TO: Downtown Burlington, Vermont. The Greyhound Bus Station, the Boston cab at the curb. Leslie pockets $44.50 given him by the cabbie. The cabbie sings, "Go Greyhound, and leave the driving to them," turns his car and heads back southward. Angie, exhausted, waves. Leslie takes her hand. As they walk slowly to the station door, Angie looks nervously over her shoulder. No murderous blue Chevy.

CUT TO: A gas station on the outskirts of White River Junction, Vermont. An innocent blue Chevy, tanking up. Three of the Seven Men surround an attendant, who says, "A Boston cab? You turkeys're outa your tree."

The Three call the other Four. "To the Home?" ask the Three. "Of course," respond the Four. Together they de-spatch the attendant. Gone the least evidence of investigation.

CUT TO: The Bus Station. Leslie and Angie sit on a stone bench. Leslie stares at a fat young man, wearing a brown suit. "Mummy? That man over there? I hate him."

Angie: "No Leslie, don't . . . don't—"

Leslie: "I can't help myself. He looks like one of the men who killed Daddy—"

Angie: "No—no—"

Then it's too late. The man grabs the front of his immense stomach, tears open his shirt and rubs his bellybutton violently, trying with friction to melt the ice that has suddenly formed there. Now the man is bouncing, up, down, up, higher and higher each time. He crashes his head against the ceiling and slams flat to the floor.

CUT TO: A pleasant house in the suburbs. In the b.g. Leslie, age six, plays in the garden. Brad says to Angie, "This force of his—he has to control it like we've learned to control ours."

"His—power—"

Brad speaks sternly. "Call it by its right name, for cat's sake." He shakes his head. "Umbilokinesis. I've been studying some research about it. The Russians have done a bunch of experiments, taking a page from Freud—"

"Crimimy, Brad, he's our little boy—"

"And in South Africa, a Dr. Willm Van Guhn has theorized that navel detrita, gathering there—"

"You mean bellybutton lint?"

"—gathered there from all over one's body contains the essence of that person's body language and the whole of his mind-set."

Angie has become profoundly depressed.

"Angie, you do understand what I'm saying, don't you?"

Angie, weak: "What."

"Our little Leslie, he can read that lint. And—more."

"Much more?"

"Yes."

"He—he can use it to make people do whatever he wants?"

"Yes."

"Then it's true. Holy crullers."

"Our little baby."

"But umbilokineses, Brad—"

"Our powers are limited. We can only make people think nice thoughts. But Leslie—"

"He can do anything."

"Yes."

"Our incredible little boy."

"Perhaps—Dr. Gorm's incredible little boy also."

"No, Brad! No!"

"I don't know what to say, Angie. I really don't."

CUT TO: The Boston cab parked in front of a late-night Burlington diner near the entrance to the interstate. Inside, the cabbie alone at a booth for four, reading the newspaper. He turns a page and glances at the entry for his birth sign, Pisces. He hums "Tea for Two." Outside, the midnight blue Chevy pulls up. Seven Men get out, enter the diner. They join the cabbie, eight in the booth. They talk. They de-spatch him, cleanly. The Seven amble from the diner, into the night. The booth is empty, silent. The waiter clears, glances at the paper. Jeanne Dixon smiles up at him.

CUT TO: A plush office. A genteel bureaucrat, Winthrop Schwartz-Bishop—called the President by allies and enemies alike—sits handsome but redfaced at his desk, yelling into a telephone. "What would they be doing in Montpelier, you dummox. Burlington! Burlington! An incident at the bus station!" The phone slams down.

Opposite squats one-armed Juan Goatherd, height four feet eleven and a half inches.

The President holds an open file, shuffles through, reads as he speaks. "Well Juan, it's impressive. A Ph.D. from Tom Smith University with a thesis on the insights of Carlos Casteñada. The piecemeal destruction of your left arm during those eight years in Vietnam. First-rate ameliorative retaliation at the seizure of your Phoenix ranch by the Casa Mesa Azul Urbliss Townhouse and Condominium Programme. I'm certain all this, taken together, is what has made you the Council's finest de-spatcher ever. And no question, your past work is of the highest quality. Now," he smiles warmly, "now we have for you the most important job of your career."

Where they meet, Goatherd's lips curl upward, a chilly grin. "All jobs are my job. I thank the winds it is summer so I may de-spatch him . . . shirtlessly."

The President stares, aghast. "How—how did you know?" His twitching eyes reveal a deepening though still controlled fear. He touches his coat jacket, as if to straighten the lapel. Close-up of his hand and a bleeper which, when activated, seals the doors of the Council for Security Matters and brings seven squads of Seven Men to his rescue. If he presses, here, lightly, twice— But he stops himself. Not now. A time to listen.

Goatherd's smile grows ever more chilly. "My greatest wish is to to stare into the boy's eyes and feel the cold. To see if it is colder than the cold in my fingers in mid-winter—my ten fingers. And when it's over I shall buy myself that pair of unborn-gnu-skin gloves I saw last week at I. Magnin."

"Juan—Juan—you already have over two hundred pairs of gloves, made of the skins and wools of all known animals, gloves of naugahyde, of rubber, of silk and of paper. Why—another pair?"

Close-up of the thermometer as the temperature in the room drops two degrees.

Goatherd says: "To keep my lost hand warm."

CUT TO: Burlington. The Cliffside Motel. A sweet couple, sixtyish, at the desk. Checking in, a sigh of relief, Angie and Leslie. The motel wife speaks kindly. "You look tired."

"That's the first nice thing anyone's said to us in a long time." Angie fills out the registration form wearily, adding, "I mean, by themselves."

"What a handsome boy. We love children. We've never been able to have any."

"How sad."

"We've been trying for forty-two years. Its gets more difficult all the time."

Leslie, glancing outside, tugs her arm. The villainous blue Chevy has pulled to a stop! Terror on Angie's face as Seven Men climb out. Each pats himself at the armpit. Angie lays her hand on Leslie's shoulder. He pulls away, gently. As she stares at him her horror increases. A small Henri (le Douanier) Rousseau smile has crept onto his face.

"Leslie, no . . ." she whispers.

The boy beams, beatific. "It's all right."

The door opens. The Seven enter, single file. The last one closes the door behind him.

The sweet motel couple are delighted by this increase in clientele.

The First Man, friendly, says, "Hello Angie, hi there Leslie." The Second reverses the greeting, "Hello Leslie, hi there Angie." Then Three through Seven say in unison, "Hi there Leslie, hello Angie." All smile with the assurance of a successful future.

The motel couple scowl. They sense a loss of customers.

(murder murder maybe murder maybe murder murder maybe maybe—)

"We'll give you a ride home," says the First.

Leslie, cold:	Your navoice tells me better. You mean the Celestial Rest Home.
The Second:	No of course not. Home to the Council.
Leslie:	You want to kill my Mummy! I know! I know!
The First:	Don't be silly. We just—
Leslie:	You are! I know! I can hear you!

And suddenly the First Man grabs his stomach, and his face freezes. Literally freezes. Then his hand tries to move from his bellybutton to his face but it cannot, it is frozen. And now he is a block of ice.

The Fifth Man draws his pistol which accidentally bumps against the frozen man. The body shatters: a heap of ice litters the floor.

"My goodness," says the motel wife.

"Umbilokinesis," says Angie.

Instantly all pistols are drawn. Immediately all hands are frozen. The Six remaining Men turn and run without order out the door. The Fifth suddenly develops agonizing chilblains, his pores seize up, the wastes of his body ooze inward, begin to poison him, then he freezes altogether. The Sixth trips, his feet have become small glacial cakes, he falls, his body an icicle. Four Men leap into the newly spacious blue Chevy— It won't start! The radiator is frozen, and now the block cracks.

Leslie steps into the open doorway, they see him, they run from the car in terror. Into the consciousness of one leaps the notion he's a cold-blooded snake, he drops to his belly and slithers toward Burlington. Two others insist on becoming cool duelists, they shoot each other at five paces, one in the mind, the other in the body. The last runs like a brushfire, trying to generate heat. Recalling he'll have to make a report he turns for a moment to inspect the devastation. A naive move: he suddenly clutches his navel, he has come to believe himself a swallow heading south for winter. He rushes to the cliff, flaps his arms, dives off head-first.

Leslie's eyes search in all directions. He spots the motel couple's car.

Angie: "No, Leslie—we'll need it!"

Leslie turns to his mother, against her, his eyes pierce.

She hugs herself to fend of the numbing bite of the frost. She whispers, "Golly, umbilikinetigellation—"

Then all cold is gone. Leslie screams. "Mu-u-u-u-mmmeee!" And faints.

CUT TO: Canada. Four hundred miles north of the Arctic Circle. A cabin on the shore of a bay. Icebergs drift about in the water. A sunny afternoon. In front of the cabin, Angie, ravishing in green organdy. Leslie, at her side, wears a bathing suit.

Angie: "Don't stay in too long, darling. The water's cold."

Leslie grins. "Not for me." He darts off, stops, turns. "You know, Mummy, I like hiding here. So what I can do goes unnoticed. I mean if I ever did it again. Which I never ever will."

She comes to her son then and hugs to her. He must not see the tears. At first they glisten, diamonds in her eyes. Quickly they run through her mascara. He hugs her in return, lets go and rushes to the shore. She waves but he doesn't look back.

In the shallow water, playing, Leslie sees a swimmer wearing a rubber wetsuit and fins. His outfit suits him like a glove. The frogman approaches. Startled, the boy's powers activate instantly. But all he can hear from the strange swimmer's navoice is: . . . The Winds and the Tides, The Magic of Tides Yet Unborn . . . The swimmer comes closer: . . . the Tides, the Magic of Winds . . . Now the man, small and with only one arm, is beside him. "Hello, little boy."

"Hello. What are you doing here."

"I'm looking for oil. Under the surface of the ocean." —the Tides, the Magic—

(no you're not, you're lying, you're—)

Leslie, aloud: "That's nice."

And Goatherd: "Would you like to dive from my shoulders?" —Yet Unborn, The Winds and—

(I mustn't, I shouldn't, who is he?)

Leslie: "Yeah, that'd be great—"

Angie appears at the cabin door. She tries to shout. The words freeze in her throat. She watches, horrified.

Leslie climbs onto the frogman's shoulders. The boy dives. The man draws a syringe from his pouch. The boy surfaces. Goatherd plunges the needle into Leslie's arm.

Now Angie screams, starts to run to the shoreline, stops: she is suddenly surrounded by Seven Men from the Council, their leader The Man Who Got Away at the Cliffside Motel.

CUT TO: Leslie, watching television. The room is small, cozy, windowless. Flowers in a vase, a large gurgling fish tank with a variety of colourful tropical species, an ever-present pussycat.

Dr. Gorm enters, carrying a pan. "Hello." His grin, an attempt at friendliness, dribbles fear. In his mind we see The President telling him: Your last chance, Gorm. With the little lint-reader. No success, and Gorm goes Home. "How are you, my boy?" No answer. "Say listen I want you to freeze this pan of water." No response. "You know what I did? Just for you? I haven't washed or changed my clothes all week. Lots of lint collected and I

(even worse the smell)

thought you might like to read it."

"No thanks."

Silence.

Gorm starts to sweat. Now or never. "All right. You co-operate or I'll make sure something really bad happens to your mother." From the corner of his mind's-eye Leslie glares at Gorm's midsection. No, nothing new there, his mother is safe, they're still trying to experiment on her too.

Gorm rubs his navel: did he imagine this or has a chill just penetrated his belly? He shivers. Perspiration dribbles from his armpits and down his back. He turns, leaves.

CUT TO: A padded cell, bright yellow. Angie has put on thirty-five pounds. She reaches for a small bottle, takes out a pill, pops it in her mouth. She thinks, then decides: she lifts a picture from the wall, notes a small spot behind it and rubs her fingernail back and forth across it, harshly.

CUT TO: A bald three-piece-suited Council for Security Matters officer tearing the phones from his head and rubbing his ears wildly.

CUT TO: Angie, bored. She starts to pop another pill— Her inner voice speaks: Stop this. Will your mind ever be able to function again? She takes the pill, stares at it, rolls it about between her fingers— And flushes it down the toilet.

CUT TO: Leslie's room. Goatherd enters, three large Mars bars in his single hand. He wears a green lead-lined T-shirt. "Hello."

Leslie stares. Silence.

"Listen, son. I desperately want to tell you something." He sets down the candy bars, lays a finger across his lips, takes Leslie by the shoulder and powerfully draws him under the fish tank: . . . The Storms and the Fishes, the Roe of Fishes Unborn, The Storms . . . "They can't hear us down here. Too much activity above."

No response. The cat wanders by. Leslie pets it, absently.

. . . The Storms . . . Fishes Unborn . . . Goatherd speaks: "Look you may not believe me, but more than anything else I want to apologize. Really."

Silence.

"When I captured you, they had me in their control. Completely. They'd implanted electrodes in my

(what is this garbage? fishes?
storms? what's going on?)

brain and in my stump. I was like a—a robot. Honest. They pulled the strings, I was their puppet. They set me up—"

The lights in the room suddenly flicker, dim, and go out.

Leslie cannot hold himself back from speaking. "What—?"

Goatherd: "Oh no, oh no, no, no!"

"Hey, you okay?"

(still all storms and fishes and roe,
can he be telling the truth—?)

"The lights. In Nam. My arms. In the dark. Each time a little more. Lights out. Cut cut. Hack hack. Oh my God!"

"Hey, take it easy—"

Leslie helps the suffering Goatherd struggle through the long dark. Five hours later the lights come back, they've shared the three candy bars, they've become friends. Leslie has decided to do as Goatherd suggests, freeze a few pans of water. What does it matter. Co-operate and they'll maybe let him go. And his Mummy. Nothing has told him different.

CUT TO: The President's office. Goatherd enters, sits. The President says, "We've just de-spatched Gorm. Tomorrow we're de-spatching Angie O'Tee."

Goatherd squints. "Don't give me information like that! I told you."

"I just thought—"

"No you didn't. White men never think. Except for—" His face fills with deep admiration. And perhaps more . . . "The boy. He thinks hard. And cold."

"My God, Goatherd—" The President reaches to his lapel, the bleeper— But stops himself.

"His cold. My cold. My cold. His cold. Tell me, Prez. What do you think could happen?"

Goatherd's smile sends hot and cold goose bumps running across the President's shoulders.

CUT TO: Leslie's room. Goatherd. A pan of water. Leslie in shallow concentration. Suddenly: the water is ice. Goatherd is delighted. "Hurrah! Hurrah!"

Leslie squints at him, grinning. His eye

(why should it matter to Juan? why—)

catches a piece of dandruff on Goatherd's shoulder. It's as though—the dandruff—not enough—it's trying to—to tell him—what?—is it he'd—what!?—more dandruff on Goatherd's head—together—together—Yes!

(no!—oh no! Mummy! Mummy!)

What?—What to do?—yes!—freeze Juan—no—wait—what'd he say—?

"I said it's getting c-c-c-oold in here—"

"Oh. Sorry. I'll shut it off—" the Power! Power— It wants to be used! Find out— Control it . . . Send it.

CUT TO: The President stepping into the yellow-padded room. "Hello Angie. We're going for a little ride."

Now. If ever in her life her mind could pull— Behind her back her fists squeeze tight. "Later. The middle of the night. At 2:15 a.m. we leave. A nondescript 198- Lincoln. Leslie will be with us. You'll be in back. In the trunk. Closed."

"But that's precisely what I meant. I love trunks. My parents travelled the vaudeville circuit, yes they did."

"Huh?"

"I'll pack us a picnic breakfast. Metracal for me. If I don't stay on my diet there's no telling—"

CUT TO: Leslie's room. The President and Angie enter, wake the boy. Silently they pass along a hallway, through a door, out. The cat follows. A garden lies peaceful before them in soft moonlight. Leslie picks up the cat, carries him. They open the Lincoln door.

From nowhere, Goatherd's invisible voice: "Leslie, put the cat down."

Silence. Leslie looks up to Angie. Her high cheekbones are outlined against the moonlit sky, her face fills with anguish. She nods. Leslie drops the cat. Goatherd shoots the cat dead.

Where is he? "You faker! You liar! They didn't put those electrodes on you!" Where is he?!

"Of course not, my lad. You saw how quickly the pussycat died? You might succeed in freezing me but I'll kill your mother first. Come here."

Now everything happens with lightning speed. Angie, out of practice, relaxes her pull on the President. Realizing the extreme danger, the President presses the bleeper in his lapel twice—Bleep! Bleep!—and grabs Angie. Leslie jerks about. On all sides lights come on. The President, relieved, smiles. Leslie, terrified, slams the Presidential navel with -10,000 degrees Fahrenheit— The President turns into two hundred ten pounds of hoarfrost. Goatherd shoots. Angie falls dead on the seat of the Lincoln. "Mummy! Mummy!" But it's too late, they'll never speak to each other again.

Leslie turns. Navels are unnecessary, the whole world is a navel, his stare deep-freezes everything within a seventy-five-foot radius: flower beds, snails and Juan Goatherd. For more than fifteen years nothing will grow here. No living thing . . .

They come now for the boy, seven Units of seven Squads of Seven Men. He freezes them at a glance, all three hundred forty-three of them. Sobbing, he gives a last hug and kiss to his mother's corpse and rushes headlong into the darkness.

CUT TO: The motel in Burlington. The sweet old couple at the desk. The door opens. Leslie enters.

"You!"

"Yes."

"Why did you come back?"

"Because—because no one was ever kind to us. Except you."

CUT TO: The old couple, at the dinner table by themselves.

She: "Is he asleep?"

He: "Yes."

She: "What'll we do?"

"Can you imagine. A thing like this perpetrated by our own Council. He's got to tell that story."

"To who? Who can he trust?"

"Well, the proper authorities—"

"He scares me. Children are so strange. If only we'd had one of our own we'd know how to deal with him."

CUT TO: The office of Stephanie Queen, writer. The door opens. Leslie comes out, Ms. Queen follows.

Ms. Queen: "And what will you do now?"

Leslie: "Well—I'll get a little older first. Then I'll finish the job."

Ms. Queen: "Oh."

LOVE AND GROCERIES

PER BRASK

Don't expect too much romance this month, his horoscope had said. "What else is new?" he thought to himself looking at cases of B.C. apples deciding which ones and how many to buy.

Brent was at the market at least twice a week to select fresh produce for his store. His business was located in a very upscale part of town but it was small and he had to compete with no less than four conveniently located supermarkets, so his way of attracting a loyal, if small, clientele was to provide the freshest possible produce and courteous service to families in his neighbourhood. Slowly approaching his late-thirties Brent had bought the store eight years ago with money his father, the president of a fair-sized furniture chain, had left him when he died.

His existence was a quiet one as he had never married and consequently had no children. His lack of children irritated his mother whose greatest wish was to become a grandmother and his lack of a wife worried the rest of the family. Perhaps something was wrong with him? In a variety of ways he attempted to allay the family's fears by inviting women friends to high holidays and special events but that hadn't seemed to satisfy their worries. Everyone in his family wished the very best for Brent, according to their understanding of the very best. And Brent really wasn't in profound disagreement with their vision of it but he did have some very intense ideals about love. And he just hadn't been able to come close to those with any woman he had dated so far. He was looking for a woman with whom he could take flights of fancy.

Brent decided on two cases of McIntosh apples and went over to look at the celery hearts. It was hard for him to focus his concentration, not because of the horoscope or because it was 6:30 a.m. but because of the dream he'd had last night. He'd dreamt that he was delivering a small box of goods to a nice bungalow not far from his store. A woman had opened the door and he'd instantly fallen in love with her and she with him and the rest is history, as they say. And that in more ways than one, because this woman (who was a widow twelve years older than himself) was a history professor at a local university. The dream had been so "real" and so dense with events that he had felt a sense of delightful exhaustion when he woke up, as if it had really happened. A very different sensation from his normal wish-fulfilment dreams. This one had been so tactile.

His concentration was off again. He realized that he'd been standing staring into space holding a celery stalk in his hand when he was brought out of his daydream by one of his female colleagues from across town passing by saying, "Hi." For a split second he thought she was the history professor of his dreams and he must have looked very disappointed when reality burst in on him because the woman said, "I see you've heard we might have a handlers' strike." And she was gone behind a stack of orange crates and so was the image of the history professor as Brent put the celery back in its place.

Brent had been to university ages ago but he'd never taken a history course and the whole experience of university had been distasteful to him. He felt it had taught him very little other than to be distrustful of the intellectual community, professors and students alike. Treat it with rubber gloves, like when you clean out a crate of rotten apples, was more or less his outlook on the university and its people. Why the hell then did she have to be a history professor? Maybe his subconscious was trying to deal with a secret fear of his? Maybe his dream was really about a sense of inadequacy he had to cope with? He'd certainly read enough novels and seen enough television and film to know that those were possible reasons. But none of them convinced him.

Brent finished his buying and drove to his store. Every female shape he passed conjured up images of the professor and it slowly started to irritate him that he couldn't get rid of the dream, and, then, whenever this irritation rose in him he began to regret it immediately.

He got his store ready for opening. He arranged his raw wood crates and stacked the fruit in rows. He cleaned the lighting equipment which gave his store a clear, bright look and he mopped the grey- and red-tiled floor. Shortly after Brent had opened the store the history professor walked through the door and he felt like he was either going to faint or throw up.

The woman standing in front of him asking for fresh bread while choosing two apples and a banana looked exactly like the woman he had dreamt about last night. Right down to the little mole on the right side of her chin. She looked fantastic.

"I'm sorry but the fresh bread doesn't arrive till after 10:00." Those were the first words he said to the woman of his dreams and never had he had a stronger wish that they wouldn't be the last. He didn't know what to do or what he could do.

"I've just moved in down the street. Do you deliver?"

He couldn't believe his ears. He answered that he certainly did and she gave him an order to be delivered after 3:30. He said that was fine for a schoolgirl came to take over for him in the store every day at 3:30 so he could make deliveries. And then it hit him just as she was about to pay for the apples and the banana. He knew what to ask: "How are things at the university?"

"How did you know that I teach there?"

"Just a lucky guess," he said.

"How very perceptive," and then with a smile he couldn't define she gave him her name and address for the delivery as his heart was quietly melting away.

"Have a good day, Professor Thompson."

"And you."

And me, indeed, Brent's entire being sang.

He got on to a late start with his deliveries in spite of all strenuous attempts to be ready to leave as soon as his help arrived. He hadn't had an unusual number of customers or more orders for delivery than normal but he'd had to repack boxes almost constantly. Whenever he had let his concentration slip away from the act of putting an order together his mind would seek out images of the history professor and he would either lose track of which order he was filling or he would start to put the wrong goods into a box. It was unbearably irritating and it was compounded by the fact that time seemed literally to stand still. All three hands on his clock were as if frozen, only moving ever so slightly when he didn't look.

Finally behind the wheel of his delivery van, Brent made a strategic decision. Rather than rushing over to her house, he would deliver the professor's groceries last, just in case. Just in case what? Well, he thought that given the events of his dream which opened by her receiving him at the door he had better leave himself without obligations. His young helper would lock up at 6:30 as usual if he hadn't returned by then.

The deliveries seemed to take forever which didn't surprise him after the slowness of things at the store. But anticipation rather than irritation was what he had to suffer now. However, when he parked his van in front of Professor Thompson's bungalow he knew it had all been worth it. There, in front of him, was the little grey stuccoed house with grey and white awnings he had seen in his dream. Very carefully he got out of the van and took out the box of groceries in exactly the same manner he'd done in his dream. Trying to remember how many steps he'd taken in his dream he moved slowly up the path to the house. Even the chimes he recognized! The door opened and a young woman of maybe twenty-two or twenty-three stood in the doorway.

After a heartbreaking silence Brent gathered his wits and said, "Is Professor Thompson in?"

"No, she left just fifteen minutes ago but I'll take care of this."

"Are you Professor Thompson's daughter?"

"No, both her kids live in the States. I'm a student of hers. A bunch of us are helping her get moved in here. Painting and stuff, you know."

"Yeah I know. Well, she can pay me another time," and he left the young woman with the groceries as he trudged back to his van. How could he have been so stupid to allow himself to get to this point? How could he have allowed himself to build up such hopes and feelings? He was angry with himself but soon he began to belittle Professor Thompson in his mind in order to comfort himself. She wasn't really that attractive; he had never really talked to her so the whole thing was just silly anyway; she was probably just a stuffy university matron. His mind wouldn't stop.

But his mental games did not work. For the next two weeks images of the professor occupied his mind whether he was asleep or not. The range and variety of loving embraces and fun-filled activities the two of them engaged in in his mind were awesome and though they did give him an uplift his lonely reality soon brought him crashing down again.

Then one day, it was a Friday, Professor Thompson walked into his store again. She was so lovely in her pleated skirt, high heels and navy blazer. There was, or so Brent dared to think, an intent in her eyes which he hoped was meant for him. She'd come to pay for her last order and to order some groceries for this afternoon.

"If you could come around 5:30 I would appreciate it. I won't be home until then."

"No problem."

"And I'd like you to bring some of these cookies. For, say, four or so dollars worth."

"Very good. Which kind in particular?"

"Surprise me!" she said and looked straight into his eyes. He could not help but feel that this was meant as a command to him and was not at all intended as a reference to the cookies.

As with his last delivery to Professor Thompson's house he took some care with his approach to her door. But he did not really expect anything this time, though he couldn't help hoping, of course. This time, however, she did open the door and she was wearing the paint-stained jeans and sweatshirt he'd seen in his dreams and she did ask him if he would be kind enough to carry the groceries into her kitchen. And she did give him a very big and meaningful smile.

"My dear Brent," she said with happy tears in her eyes, "how long you've been about it." And then she kissed him on the cheek.

Every step and every word had been exactly as in his very first dream about her. And this was only the beginning!

Acknowledgements

Some of the stories in this collection have appeared as follows:

"Sense" first appeared in *Descant*, Winter 1985/86; "On Cheemy Pond" first appeared in *Discours Social/Social Discours*, Winter, 1988; "The Year the Leaves Were Smaller" first appeared in *Boston Review*, December 1987; and "Skull" first appeared in *Matrix*, Fall 1989.

Photograph by Peter Tittenberger.

Per Brask

Born in Denmark, Per Brask has lived in Canada since 1975. He is an Associate Professor in the Department of Theatre and Drama at the University of Winnipeg, where he has taught since 1982. Over the years he has directed countless plays at theatres in Denmark, Manitoba, Quebec, and Ontario, as well as television dramas. He has published short stories, poems and plays in several Canadian journals, including *Border Crossings*, *The Malahat Review*, *Arts Manitoba*, *Prairie Fire* and *NeWest Review*. A chapbook, *Power/lessness* was published by Turnstone in 1987. Per has also published several pieces of drama criticism and translated many plays from Danish to English. Previously, he has collaborated with George Szanto on the radio dramas, "Bagman" and "Voices of Canada" which were produced by CBC Radio. Per Brask is married to Carol Matas, who is the author of several novels for young people.

Photograph by Peter Wolheim.

George Szanto

Originally from Northern Ireland, George Szanto has lived in England, Germany, France, the United States and Canada. He currently divides his time between Montréal and Mexico. He is a professor in Graduate Communications at McGill University. Over the years, he has published many stories in journals and magazines in England, Canada and the U.S. His short story "How Ali Cran Got His Name" was a finalist in the CBC Literary Competition in 1986 and winner of the Silver Foundation Prize of the National Magazine Awards for 1987. He has also published several plays, the most recent being "The Great Chinchilla War" (Playwrights Canada, 1983). His novel, *Not Working* (St. Martin's, 1982; MacMillan, 1983; Avon, 1984) was a finalist for the *Books in Canada* Award for First Novels. *The Underside of Stones*, a story cycle will be published by McClelland & Stewart in 1990. Currently he is at work on two more novels.

Fiction from Coteau Books

Other fiction from Coteau Books is listed below. You may order any of these titles from your favorite bookstore. For a complete catalogue of publications—fiction, poetry, drama, criticism, humour and children's literature—please write to 209-1945 Scarth Street, Regina, Saskatchewan S4P 2H2.

The McCourt Fiction Series

Bonnie Burnard, *Women of Influence*. McCourt Fiction Series 5. Named best first published book in the Caribbean-Canada region for the 1989 Commonwealth Writers Prize. $21.95 (cl), $8.95 (pbk), Fall 1988, second printing 1989.

Dianne Warren, *The Wednesday Flower Man*. McCourt Fiction Series 4. Witty and whimsical fiction. $8.95 (pbk), Fall 1987.

Connie Gault, *Some of Eve's Daughters*. McCourt Fiction Series 3. Unusual stories in an eclectic range of styles. $8.95 (pbk), Spring 1987.

Robert Currie, *Night Games*. McCourt Fiction Series 1. Poignant stories about adolescence in the fifties. $7.00 (pbk), Fall 1983.

More fiction from Coteau Books

Per Brask and George Szanto, *Duets*. Fourteen short stories, the product of a unique collaboration. $8.95 (pbk), Fall 1989.

Craig Grant, *The Last India Overland*. An enthralling novel set in 1978. $7.95 (pbk), Fall 1989.

Sky High: Stories from Saskatchewan. Twenty-four stories from Saskatchewan writers, edited by Geoffrey Ursell. $5.95 (pbk), Fall 1988.

Pat Krause, *Best Kept Secrets.* Award-winning stories from a Regina writer. $21.95 (cl), $8.95 (pbk), Fall 1988.

Veronica Eddy Brock, *The Valley of Flowers: A Story of a TB Sanatorium.* A popular novel about the experiences of a young girl confined to a TB sanatorium during the forties. $5.95 (pbk), Fall 1987, second printing 1988.

The Old Dance: Love Stories of One Sort or Another. Thirty short stories that examine love, edited by Bonnie Burnard. $4.95 (pbk), Fall 1986.

Sharon Butala, *Queen of the Headaches.* This collection was nominated for the Governor-General's fiction award in 1985. $6.95 (pbk), Fall 1985, second printing 1989.

More Saskatchewan Gold. Imaginative and masterful short stories from Saskatchewan writers, edited by Geoffrey Ursell. $4.95 (pbk), Fall 1984.

Barbara Sapergia, *Foreigners.* A sensitive portrayal of a Romanian immigrant family on the Prairies at the turn of the century. $4.95 (pbk), Fall 1983.